Three moments in time,
three very different tall tales.

First published by OneTree House Ltd, New Zealand

Text © David Hill, 2021

9781990035029

All rights reserved. No part of this publication may be reproduced, stored in a retrieval system or transmitted in any form or by any means, electronic, mechanical, photocopying, recording or otherwise, without the prior permission of the publisher.

Cover art and internal illustrations by Lisa Allen

Cover concept: OneTree House

Typesetting: 11/21.3pt Diaria Pro

Printed: New Zealand, YourBooks

10 9 8 7 6 5 4 3 2 1   1 2 3 4 5 6/2

Three Scoops

Stories by
DAVID HILL

With illustrations by
LISA ALLEN

OneTree HOUSE

CONTENTS

Coming Home	7
I Wish	99
Strange Meeting	209

Coming Home

ONE

Harry ran through the back gate and into the paddock. The morning was blue and bright. Snow glowed white on the mountains.

His heart beat fast, and he couldn't wait to tell Blaze. Where was his horse?

There – waiting by the barn, as usual. Blaze saw his master coming and tossed his head. He stamped one hoof, and whinnied.

Harry stopped, and gazed proudly at the young animal. He saw the glossy, brown coat, long powerful legs, the white 'blaze' mark on the forehead.

The best horse in all of New Zealand! he thought. No other steed was as fast and brave and strong as

Blaze. And now they were off together on a wonderful adventure.

He reached his horse and leaned against the shining neck. Blaze whinnied softly again and pushed his head against his master's chest.

'My brave Blaze,' Harry whispered. 'You'll never believe where you and I are going!'

* * *

Great brown eyes watched the young man. His pal seemed to be listening. Harry laughed, and stroked the long mane.

'We've ridden all over Mother and Father's farm,' he said. 'You've carried me up the steepest hills and down the most dangerous gullies. We've crossed flooded rivers together.'

He stroked the mane once more. Blaze pushed his head closer against his master's chest.

'We've found lost sheep and carried them home on your saddle,' Harry went on. 'You've stood as steady as a young tree while I shot wild pigs from your back. No other horse could be so calm and clever.'

COMING HOME

He stared at the blue and white mountains. 'Now we're going on a great adventure together. We're going on a ship, all the way to South Africa. We're going to fight in a war, beside our British comrades.'

The young horse flicked his tail, and Harry smiled. 'Yes, we're going to beat those rebels who are causing trouble over there. Men and horses from all across New Zealand are joining the British to help. We'll travel to a strange new land and do exciting things. We'll meet more horses than you've ever seen, and you'll be the strongest and bravest of them all!'

The tall pine tree by the barn rustled in a breeze. Sheep bleated to one another, and birds darted through the bright air. Harry spoke more quietly.

'A telegram from the Army arrived before breakfast. Mother wept when she saw it. Father shook his head, but he understands. We have to go, Blaze. We have to help our British friends against these rebels. "Boers" they're called. What a strange name. I wonder what they're like?'

He held Blaze's mane in one hand and swung himself up onto the glossy, brown back. 'Every other soldier will wish he had a horse like you. You'll be the greatest in the whole war!'

Blaze tossed his head once more and began trotting around the paddock. Harry pressed his heels against the strong sides. Blaze broke into a canter, legs flowing across the ground.

Sheep lifted their woolly faces and stared. Magpies squawked from the pine tree. Harry pulled gently on the mane till Blaze slowed and stopped.

Young horse and young man stood in the bright morning, facing the silent mountains.

'I wonder what it will be like to ride with bullets flashing past and shells exploding,' Harry said. 'We may have to charge against men who are shooting at us, my Blaze. I hope I can be brave. I know you will be. You have a bigger heart than any horse I've ever known.'

He slid from the high, brown back. Blaze turned his head and rubbed it against his master's shoulder.

COMING HOME

The white patch on his forehead shone in the sun.

Harry gazed at the farmhouse behind the hedge. Smoke rose from its kitchen chimney.

'We have to come back safely, Blaze. It will break Mother and Father's hearts if we don't.'

He patted Blaze's neck and felt the muscles ripple beneath the coat. 'People say South Africa is a beautiful place. There are wide plains with antelopes and even lions. There are high, rocky hills, too.'

He stepped back and gazed proudly at his horse again. 'We will come back safely, my friend. We can do anything together!'

Harry gave Blaze a last pat. 'We leave a week from tomorrow, on the train. We take your saddle and bridle. But today – today we ride out to fix fences on the top paddock, my boy. There's work to be done!'

* * *

Blaze watches as Harry goes into the barn. He doesn't understand the words his master has spoken, but he can hear the excitement in the young man's voice, feel it in his body. It makes Blaze excited, too.

He tosses his head again, jumps a few steps sideways. The magpies squawk once more in the pine tree, and he snorts at the silly creatures.

His master comes out with the saddle, lays it over the wooden rail, starts to polish it. Blaze watches.

Soon they will ride somewhere on the farm. The two of them, as they do so often. Up the steep paddocks towards the bush and mountains, with hawks sailing above. Or along beside the river, where fantails dart and skim. As long as his master is with him, Blaze will be happy.

The young man is rubbing so hard at the saddle, that the leather glows like Blaze's own coat.

He moves towards Blaze, carrying the saddle. Blaze steps forward to meet him. Something special is going to happen soon. He doesn't know what it is, but as long as his master is with him, he will be all right. Together, they can do anything.

TWO

It was eight days later. The weather had changed. The morning was dark, and a thin rain soaked down. Water dripped from the pine tree. The sheep and magpies were silent.

Blaze stood waiting at the front gate of the farmhouse. A saddle lay across his back, with two bags of clothes and food hanging from it.

Harry was on the verandah, arms around his mother. She was crying.

'I'll be all right, Ma,' he kept saying. 'I'll be careful. Blaze will look after me.'

The young man's father shook his hand. 'He's a fine young horse, son. One of the best. You're one of the best, too. Now go and do your duty.'

Harry swung up into the saddle. 'Goodbye,' he murmured.

His parents raised their hands. 'Goodbye, son. God bless you and keep you safe.'

Horse and rider set off along the rough track. Harry didn't look back. After a while, he spoke quietly. 'I knew war would be an adventure, Blaze. I didn't know it would mean such sadness, too.'

The rain drifted down as they rode on.

* * *

The railway station was an hour's ride away. It was just a small wooden shed beside the metal lines. Two other young men sat inside, while a grey horse and a black horse stood nearby.

'Hello, Ted,' called Harry. 'Hello, Dick.'

His friends from the local farms said hello. Harry lifted the bags from his saddle and carried them into the shed. Blaze began nibbling grass beside the other horses.

The three men sat and talked. 'How long before

COMING HOME

our ship sails for South Africa?' wondered Dick. 'I can't wait.'

'How long before we see some fighting against those Boer rebels?' Ted asked. 'Think of us all, charging at them on our horses. It'll be wonderful!'

Half an hour passed. The horses lifted their heads and pricked up their ears.

Then the friends heard it, too. A faint chugging and puffing sound. 'The train,' said Harry.

The noise grew louder. A steam whistle blew, making Ted and Dick's horses rear, and tug at their reins. Blaze stood quietly.

A second whistle, and the train appeared around a corner, black smoke pouring from its chimney. It stopped beside the shed, and a soldier jumped down.

'Hello, lads. Good to see you.' He checked a sheet of paper in his hand. 'Dick Smale, Ted Ratana and Harry Barton?' The three friends nodded.

'Good,' the soldier said. 'Help me with this ramp, and we'll get your steeds on board.'

The black and grey horses didn't want to climb the wooden ramp into the railway wagon. They snorted, rolled their eyes, stood shaking. Ted and Dick pulled at their reins, but they wouldn't move.

'Come on, Blaze,' Harry said.

He took the brown horse's bridle in one hand and walked slowly up the ramp. Blaze followed. He stopped at the top, sniffed the strange smell of the wagon, then stepped inside.

'Well done!' called the soldier. 'That's a fine horse you have there.'

'Best in the world,' Harry told him. 'Except for these two, of course.'

He watched as Dick's grey and Ted's black horse came up the ramp. They were still nervous, ears flicking and eyes rolling, but Blaze snorted gently to them from inside the wagon, and they kept moving.

'Good work, lads,' the soldier said when all three steeds were inside, and the ramp was lifted up. 'There's room for you all in the carriage.'

'I'll stay with Blaze for a bit,' Harry said. 'You blokes go on.'

Dick grinned. 'You and that horse. Sometimes I think you can read each other's minds.'

* * *

The train started off. The wagon jerked, and the other two horses jumped in fright.

'It's all right,' Harry told them.

He watched as Blaze rubbed his head against the black and grey coats in turn, till they were quiet. 'You can certainly read their minds, pal!' he laughed. They clattered past paddocks and farmhouses. Rain dripped from dark stretches of bush. The clouds hung low. Harry leaned on the windowsill of the wagon and stared out. He thought of his friends' words. How long till they sailed? How long till they were fighting in the war? It would be such a great adventure.

The wagon jerked again, so hard that Harry almost fell. The clattering changed to a *bang-bang-bang!* The bush vanished, and there was nothing but air all around them. They were steaming over a high bridge, with a river far below.

That gave me a fright, he thought. The *bang-bang-bang!* got louder. The wagon jolted even harder. And the two other horses went mad.

They screamed in terror. Their bodies bucked and leaped. Their hooves flung out in all directions, crashing into the wooden sides of the wagon. Harry threw himself into a corner. If one of those hooves hit him, it could break his arm or leg.

'Easy!' he called. 'Easy!' He stretched out an arm, trying to stroke the terrified animals. Their eyes rolled. Froth flew from their mouths. The black horse saw Harry's hand reaching towards him. Its great teeth chomped at his fingers, and Harry ducked away.

'Easy!' he called again. But the two frightened animals kept plunging and kicking. Any second now, they'd smash down the wagon's wooden side. The train was still jolting across the bridge with the river's rocky bed 100 feet below. If the black and grey tried to escape, they'd fall to their deaths.

Blaze stood staring at the other horses. His body trembled. His dark eyes rolled. Oh, no, thought Harry. If he goes crazy, too ...

The young man stretched out a hand again. Then he stopped. Blaze was stepping forward, slowly and steadily, pressing against the two terrified steeds. The black tried to kick. The grey flung its head towards Blaze, teeth bared.

But Blaze ignored the grey and kept moving. He pushed the other two backwards, pressing his powerful body against them, till all three horses were close together in a corner of the wagon. The black and grey shook and panted, but they stopped kicking.

Blaze rubbed his nose against their coats. He snorted softly in their ears. After a few minutes, the other two stood quietly. Their bodies were wet with sweat, but they seemed calm.

The sound of the train's wheels had changed

back to a clatter. Trees and paddocks appeared once more. A herd of cows stood staring.

Harry shook his head. He walked across to where Blaze stood, still pressed against the other two horses.

'Oh, my boy!' he whispered. 'You are amazing! As long as you and I are together, we can win this war by ourselves!'

* * *

The train steamed on, through the wet day and into the night. Each time it stopped at a little station for more men and horses, Harry watched the new animals being loaded into other wagons. They were good, strong steeds, but none of them could match Blaze.

He sat in the carriage for a few hours. The young men listened to the soldier as he told them how they would spend time training in Wellington before they sailed.

'These Boers are tough fighters. You lads have to become as smart and rugged as they are.'

COMING HOME

Next time the train stopped, Harry went back to the wagon with their three horses. The black and grey were quiet. Blaze's ears pricked up when he saw his master. He pushed his glossy head against the young man's chest again.

Harry smiled, and stroked the strong, brown neck. 'I'm so lucky to have you, my friend. Whatever happens, we must stick together.'

* * *

Blaze has never seen such a thing. A great wooden box on iron wheels. His master leads him up a wooden ramp into it. It smells like the barn at home.

When the hissing and clattering noise starts, and the big box begins jerking along, his heart jumps. The other two horses pant and shake, but his master is there, and Blaze knows the young man will look after him.

He is afraid when the bang-bang-bang! comes. He wants to crash out of the box and gallop away. His whole body goes stiff with fear. He hears the black and grey scream, sees them buck and twist. He wants to do so, too.

But he must protect his master. He holds back the frightened animals, keeps their flying hooves away from the young man. He will do anything for his master.

When he is left alone with the other horses, he grows nervous. Where is the young man he loves? Should he try to find him? But how?

After a long time, his master comes back. But Blaze still worries. This is a strange place. Something different is going to happen; he still has that feeling.

Whatever happens, he and the young man must be together. Together, wherever they are.

THREE

Harry's Army Company spent two weeks in a camp outside the city. Dozens of men lived in rows of Army tents, while their horses were kept in corrals with high wooden rails.

Harry visited Blaze whenever he could. He brushed the shiny, brown coat, patted his steed's neck, talked to him. He laughed when Blaze sniffed at the khaki uniform Harry now wore and tried to lick the shining, brass buttons.

'Not long now, chum. Not long till we're off together on our adventure.'

An Army blacksmith checked Blaze's iron horseshoes. 'You did a good job here,' he told Harry. The young man smiled. 'A great horse needs great hooves.'

The training was hard. They practised galloping towards an imaginary enemy, bent low over their saddles. They learned to ride in long lines, with gaps between each horse. That made them harder for any enemy to hit.

They were given Army rifles, and lay on the ground, shooting at distant targets, while their horses stood behind them, hidden in a gulley. 'That's how we'll do it against the Boers,' a sergeant told them.

When the first rifles cracked, some horses bucked, and tried to run away. The soldiers looking after them had to hang onto the reins.

'That big, brown steed of yours never even blinked,' one soldier told Harry. 'He's a wonderful beast.' Harry smiled again.

Finally, the whole Company practised a charge with rifles. Fifty men and horses at a time hurtled at top speed towards a line of bushes. Hooves drummed; glossy bodies flew forward; great lungs strained and panted.

Crouched over their saddles, Harry and the others saw the ground rushing past beneath them. 'Aim!' yelled the sergeant, riding in the middle of the line.

Harry pulled his rifle from the long leather 'bucket' on Blaze's heaving side. He gripped the reins with one hand, pointed the heavy weapon at one of the bushes ahead.

'Fire!' All along the charging line, shots rang out. *Blam! Blam-Blam!* Some horses reared and whinnied. Some lurched sideways.

Beside Harry, a white horse plunged and bucked, while its rider fought to hold on. Further away, another one crashed into its neighbour, and a soldier fell from the saddle. Men shouted at their mounts, and rifles thudded to the ground.

Blaze charged straight on. 'You beauty!' Harry heard himself yelling. 'Oh, you beauty! It's just like hunting pigs at home!'

As they rode back, horses snorting and sweating, the sergeant moved his own big, grey steed over beside Harry. 'Well done, Private Barton. That's a brave fellow you have there.'

Harry patted Blaze's neck. 'You and me, old pal. Together, we can face the whole Boer Army!'

* * *

They practised again and again, till even the most nervous horses were used to the *blam!* of rifle fire. Some still snorted and trembled. Still none was as steady as Blaze. 'Wouldn't mind having that horse of yours, Harry,' soldiers said.

Harry laughed, and shook his head. 'I don't know what I'd do without him.'

Then the news came. They were going to sail for South Africa in four days time.

Two mornings later, the whole Company paraded through the streets to the wharves. A band played, while people waved handkerchiefs, clapped and cheered. Union Jack flags hung from lamp posts and buildings.

Harry felt the powerful body stepping quietly beneath him. He wished his mother and father could see them now. He and his faithful chum were on their way to such an adventure.

On the wharf, the horses were put in more big corrals with their high, wooden rails. Some of them shifted nervously and kept snorting. Harry felt Blaze staring after him as he walked away.

'I'll be back to see you soon, pal!' he called. 'Don't worry.'

But he wasn't able to see his horse much during the next few days. He and other soldiers were kept busy, loading supplies onto the troopship beside the wharf.

They began lifting horses on board from another corral. The steeds rose through the air in huge nets, with their legs dangling from the bottom. One at a time, they were lowered onto the ship's deck, and led to the stalls that had been built for them.

Horses kicked and struggled, or tried to bite the

men taking them out of the net. Blaze will be brave about this, Harry told himself.

When he did have a few spare minutes, he hurried to see his horse. Blaze whinnied, pressed through the others in the corral, and pushed his head against Harry's chest.

'It's all right, chum,' Harry told him. 'I know you're missing me. It's a strange place, with strange things happening. Soon we'll be together on the troopship. It'll be all right then.'

But he felt his horse trembling as he left.

* * *

That night, Harry slept on the troopship. He was in a cabin with Ted and four other soldiers.

On deck, horses whinnied. He could hear others in the corral on the wharf. They sounded nervous, stamping and snorting.

Blaze and the others in his corral would be lifted on board in the morning. He and his horse would be together again. Everything will be all right then, Harry told himself, as he drifted off to sleep.

COMING HOME

He dreamed. There were banging noises. The Boers were attacking them! Wood cracked, and men cried out.

He jerked awake as a soldier burst into the cabin. 'Your horse is gone!' he shouted at Harry. 'He kicked his way out of the corral, and he's vanished. Nobody knows where he is!'

*   *   *

Blaze hates the wooden rails that shut him in. On his master's farm, he can roam free, but here, he has to stand with so many strangers. Most of them are frightened. They snort and bite. He longs for his master to come, to take him out so they can ride away.

It was all right before, when he and the other horses galloped across the open ground. Figures in khaki clothes shouted, but Blaze heard only his master's voice.

Even when the Blam! Blam! burst out around him, he wasn't afraid. He has heard those noises often, when they ride across the farm and chase the wild pigs that try to eat the gardens.

But now he is shut up in this place, with salt-smelling water all around. A huge steel shape rises up nearby. Smoke pours from it, and men in khaki move on it. Is his master there? Why doesn't he come more often? Should Blaze go to him?

This afternoon, he saw other horses being lifted up into the sky, their legs kicking in the air. Then they disappeared.

Will that happen to him? He must find his master. They must get home, to their mountains and rivers.

It is night time now. The other horses keep moving around. Blaze stands, eyes searching for one young man. He cannot see him anywhere. Has he gone forever?

Suddenly, Blaze can't bear it any longer. His powerful legs lash out at the rails. His hooves smash into them, once, twice. The other horses cry out and lurch away. Blaze kicks again, with all his strength till the top rail shatters and falls.

COMING HOME

One leap, and he is out of the corral. He must find his master. Men are shouting, running towards him. He has to get away, tell his master they must go home.

His eyes search on all sides. His nostrils are stretched wide. As fast as he can, before any of the shouting men can reach him, he gallops into the darkness.

FOUR

Right up until the hour they sailed, Harry hoped he would find where Blaze had gone.

Their Company's officer sent him and Ted to search for the young horse. Ted rode his black steed. Harry had a chestnut-coloured Army mare, that seemed slow and clumsy after his fast, young friend.

They rode along the other wharves. They searched the beach. Harry kept calling Blaze's name, and whistling for him as they rode. But there was no sign.

A few people thought they had heard hooves galloping past in the night. 'It was going so fast!' one woman told Harry and Ted. 'I couldn't believe it was just a horse.'

COMING HOME

They rode right to the edge of town, where farms began. Other horses stood in paddocks or pulled carts along the shingle roads but there was no Blaze.

'Time to head back, pal,' Ted said. 'Don't worry. Someone will find Blaze and look after him. The Army has lots of spare horses. You'll still be able to fight, along with our boys.'

Harry said nothing. But he knew no Army horse could be as good as his faithful friend. Suddenly, they had been torn apart. With Blaze, he could do anything, but now he felt afraid.

He scribbled a letter to his parents, telling them what had happened, and asking them to send any news of Blaze.

The ship sailed that afternoon. Soldiers packed the decks and ladders. Crowds on the wharf cheered, and another band played.

Harry stood, watching and hoping that Blaze would appear. If he saw his horse, he'd rush ashore. He'd even dive into the sea and swim to the wharf.

No strong, young shape came. After a while, Harry turned and went down to his cabin.

* * *

The voyage to South Africa took three weeks. Harry helped look after the other horses. He fed them and brushed them. He led them on walks around the deck, to keep them fit.

When they saw the sea flowing past, some of them were still frightened. They shivered and stamped. If the troopship rocked in rough waves, they whinnied with fear.

Harry talked to them. He stroked them and blew softly on them. They all became quieter when he was near.

'You know horses, Private Barton,' the sergeant told him. 'Pity about your own one.'

Harry was silent. He thought about Blaze all the time. Where could his pal be? Who would look after him? Would he be all right?

He still could hardly believe Blaze was gone. They'd never been apart like this before. When the war was over, and he came home, he would find his faithful horse. Somehow, some time, they were going to be together again.

* * *

The Army training carried on during the voyage. The troops practised rifle shooting at a white float towed behind the ship. Harry heard horses bucking when the shots rang out.

They did physical exercises. They cleaned their uniforms. Māori soldiers taught them how to do a haka. 'That'll scare those Boers,' Dick grinned.

Halfway through the voyage, two horses fell sick. Harry helped nurse them both, covering them with blankets, giving them water. One got better, but the other died.

Its body was lowered over the side and dropped into the sea. Harry saw its owner standing and saluting. He felt tears in his own eyes.

Once more, he thought of Blaze. Where was his dear friend?

When I come home, I'll find him, Harry promised

himself once more. I'll search all over New Zealand if I have to. I'll find him, and we'll never be apart again.

* * *

Finally, they reached South Africa. Long, grey warships lay offshore, gun barrels pointing towards the land. A range of low, brown hills stretched away inland.

At the wharf next to their own troopship, another vessel was unloading huge artillery guns. Harry and his friends watched as cranes lowered the enormous weapons onto the ground.

'Those things can hit a target 10 miles away!' someone said.

'The Boers haven't got a chance,' another voice said, as teams of horses began to haul the guns away.

Harry had almost forgotten the enemy they were going to fight. All he could think about was Blaze.

Soldiers in khaki marched past along the wharf, rifles over their shoulders. The men on Harry's ship cheered and waved.

COMING HOME

Then it was their turn. Horses squealed in terror as nets swung them over the side. Hands seized them, calmed them down. One of those horses would probably be his, thought Harry. He hoped it would be good enough to carry him through any battles, We'll do the best we can, he decided.

The men stepped down the gangway, carrying their rifles and packs. 'Right, lads,' the sergeant called. 'We've got a five-mile march to Base Camp. Then you'll find out how you're going to beat these Boers.'

The troops cheered again. Harry didn't. He wondered if he could still be a soldier without the friend he had trusted for so long. Yet again, he wished with all his heart that Blaze was safe.

* * *

For two days, Blaze hides behind a big, empty building. Its windows are broken. It's full of rubbish. He hears rats running across its floors.

Nobody comes. He waits and hopes his master will somehow find him. He sniffs the air. A couple of times, he whinnies softly. Then he stops. Other people might hear. Other people might come and take him far away. Then he will never see the man he loves.

On the third night, he moves out into the silent street. The sky glitters with stars. A breeze brings the smell of trees and grass.

He will go there, find a safe place, like the farm he knows, and wait there for his master.

Slowly, quietly, he begins moving through the dark town. His hooves clip-clop faintly on the ground. The houses are all still. Nobody moves. If any person tries to stop him, he will run for the friendly smells ahead.

He tries to understand where his master can be. Something must have happened to him. They have never been apart like this before. Blaze knows he must do everything he can to bring them together once more.

The night goes on. He moves carefully. His ears are pricked up, his nostrils stretch wide, scenting the strange smells, hoping to find the one he knows best of all. It isn't there.

The houses are mostly gone, now. Paddocks and fences stretch on both sides. A horse whinnies to him from nearby. Blaze stays silent.

A picture is growing in his mind. A picture with snowy mountains, a barn, a big pine tree. He will be safe there. He will find his master there.

Ahead of him, the sky grows pale. Morning is near. He must hide. Hide, and then decide what to do.

FIVE

After four days in Base Camp, Harry's company and their horses moved up towards the Front.

'The Front?' Ted asked when he heard the word.

'The front of our army, lad,' their sergeant said. 'The front of the Boer army, too. Where the fighting is.' The men fell silent.

Harry had been given an Army horse, as he expected. It was grey and white, with strong legs and a broad head. But the moment he rode it, he knew it wasn't as quick as Blaze.

'I'll look after you,' he told it. But all the time, he thought of another, glossier steed.

The days were burning hot. The troops wore hats

with flaps of cloth at the back and sides to keep the sun off them.

But the nights were freezing cold. Harry shivered under his Army blanket. Some nights, he and other soldiers walked around, stamping their feet to try and keep warm.

He went to the corral and talked to his Army horse. The grey-and-white was friendly enough, but it didn't hurry to him or push its nose into his chest, the way Blaze did.

A train carried them and their horses for five hours up towards the Front. A low, bare plain lay on either side. A few rocky hills rose. To Harry they looked so old, as if they had stood there since the beginning of time. There were hardly any trees, just clumps of low bushes.

The train stopped to take on water. *Crrummp, Crrummp*. Men stared at one another as a dull thumping noise sounded far ahead. Horses shifted and snorted nervously.

'It's artillery,' a man said. 'We're getting near.'

They began to stop more often, especially if the artillery sounded louder. Then they would move on again. In one place, other soldiers in khaki were lifting saddles onto their horses beside the railway. They carried rifles over their shoulders.

Harry knew his heart was beating faster. If only Blaze were here.

Then they stopped and didn't move. Wooden ramps clattered down. Their sergeant came along past the wagons. 'Get down, lads. Find your horses.'

After the horses were unloaded, and saddled, they rode slowly forward for about a mile, till a low rise of ground lay ahead of them. The artillery was louder now. They heard a different sound – the *Blam! Blam!* of rifles. Men were fighting, not far ahead.

They checked saddles, made sure reins and bridles were fitted tightly, that the leather bucket for their rifle was firmly in place.

Then they waited. The burning sun scorched down. Big, black flies stung and bit. Up ahead, the *crrummp* of artillery and the *Blam! Blam!* of rifles kept on.

'What are we waiting for?' Dick muttered. 'When are we going to do something?'

Right then, they heard galloping hooves. A sweating horse came flying over the low rise in front. A soldier threw himself from the saddle. He hurried up to the Company Officer and saluted. Then he began talking and pointing.

'Mount up!' the officer called. 'Attack formation!'

They swung up into their saddles and spread out. Harry's grey-and-white horse stood solidly. Harry licked his lips.

Their officer turned his horse to face the Company. 'The Boers are dug in behind a line of bushes 400 yards in front. We're going to drive them out. Any minute now, our artillery will stop. When I give the signal, we'll go up that rise and charge. Good luck, boys!'

They formed up in a long line, all facing forward, all listening and waiting. Dick was next to Harry, on his grey horse. 'Here we go, chum,' he grinned at Harry.

A sudden silence. The huge artillery guns had stopped. Their officer lifted his arm. 'Charge!'

Men cheered. Horses neighed. They thundered up the rise in front and hurtled across the low plain.

Harry glimpsed the line of bushes, away in front. 'Go!' he shouted to his Army horse. It pounded on, but other horses were already ahead. 'Go!' shouted Harry again.

Peee-u-u-u! Something whipped past him. Another one. *Peee-u-u-u!* Over to his left, a horse staggered and fell. Its rider tumbled to the ground. Bullets, Harry realised. They're shooting at us.

He heard the crack of rifles in front and beside him. Both sides were firing. He snatched his own rifle from its bucket, aimed it at the bushes ahead. *Blam!* His horse leaped sideways. 'Steady!' Harry yelled. 'Steady'

Noises roared all around him. Bullets whipped and rifles cracked. Hooves pounded, horses whinnied and snorted, men yelled and cheered. *Blam!* Harry fired again. The bushes seemed to be rushing nearer. Shapes were moving in them. The enemy. He aimed again and fired. *Blam!*

A new sound, from the Boer positions. *Blam-blam-blam-blam!* Horses on his right bucked and tried to turn away. A man fell, lay still on the ground. *Blam-blam-blam-blam!* Machine-gun, Harry realised. They've got a machine-gun!

His Army horse stumbled suddenly. It screamed and half fell. Harry saw the blood pouring from its shoulder. A Boer bullet had hit.

'Go!' he yelled. But the horse lurched again, then sank to its knees. Its head tossed; froth flew from its mouth.

Harry threw himself from the saddle. Blood streamed from the horse's left shoulder. A bullet had gone straight through it. The animal moaned and panted.

'Down!' Harry tugged at the reins. 'Down!' The horse sank on its side. Its breath jerked. Its frightened eyes rolled. Harry flung himself on the ground beside it.

Ahead of them his Company raced on, shouting and cheering. Beyond the bushes, figures in dark clothes were running, leaping onto horses and galloping away. The enemy were retreating.

Harry crouched beside his wounded steed, patting and talking to it. 'You did well. You're a brave boy.' Brave, but not fast, and not strong. Blaze would have led the whole Company in that charge.

I wonder where my pal is, Harry thought again. This was going to be our great adventure together. Now I just want to get home and find him. And I will find you, Blaze. I'll find you wherever you are and I'll never leave you again.

* * *

A clump of trees grow at the edge of a farm. Blaze hides there, while days and nights pass. Sometimes the sun glows. Sometimes rain falls.

One day, an icy wind slashes, and hail beats down. Blaze shivers under the trees. He remembers the barn where he would be warm and dry in such weather. He remembers his master bringing an extra blanket to put over him, laughing and saying, 'You old softie!' He waits and waits for the young man to come here.

People move in the paddocks not far away. Blaze stays hidden. They may catch him and drag him off to another place with wooden rails like the last one. Or they may lift him up in one of those nets and take him far from his home.

At night, he comes out and eats the rough grass through the paddock fences. The white shapes of sheep bleat at him. Cows lift their heads and watch.

One dark night, another horse is in the paddock. It comes over to Blaze, snorts, rubs noses with him across the fence. It's friendly, but Blaze wants only one true friend, and there is no sign of him.

His picture of the barn, the mountains and pine tree seems to grow brighter in his mind. His home. His master's home, too. Should he ...

The only grass he can reach is thin and dry. The

tree leaves are sour. He feels hungry all the time.

Another night, he moves along the fence closer to the farmhouse. Suddenly, a dog starts to bark. Blaze hears its chain rattling. He trots back to the trees, as quickly and quietly as he can.

Next morning, he sees a man standing in the paddock, looking all around. The man stares towards where Blaze is hiding and starts to walk in his direction. Blaze shivers. Then the man turns and moves away.

But Blaze understands. He isn't safe here. And his master isn't coming.

So the next night he leaves the trees and heads away from the farm. He follows a track that leads along beside a creek.

Stars glitter above. Somehow, he knows which way to go. He heads to the mountains. To the pine tree and barn and his own paddocks. That's the place he must find. The place where he hopes to find the master he loves.

His stomach is empty. But he cannot stop to eat.

COMING HOME

He lifts his head, and its white patch glimmers in the starlight. He goes on.

SIX

The other soldiers in Harry's Company kept talking about their charge at the enemy. 'See those Boers run! We showed them!'

Their sergeant shook his head. 'They're tough. They vanish and then they attack when you don't expect it. We need to be careful.'

Harry stayed quiet while the others talked. He'd been part of the charge, but he hadn't really done anything. If he'd been on Blaze, he'd have been at the front, sending the enemy fleeing.

His grey-and-white Army horse had been sent back to Base Camp in the train, for its shoulder to heal. Harry has been given another horse: a lean young animal with a chestnut coat.

COMING HOME

It is fast, but full of nerves and twitches. It jumps and rears at any noise. Every day, Harry remembers calm Blaze. Every day, he thinks of his pal; tells himself how he will find that pal again.

His Company set up camp where the Boers had been, and sent out patrols to search for any enemy. The enemy might attack from any side, their officer said; they had to check in every direction.

For three days, they rode across the stony ground, through stands of thorny bushes and dry trees. They saw farms with burned houses. Cattle stood near empty barns.

There was no sign of the enemy. Only their own patrols – soldiers in khaki on horseback, belts of ammunition across their bodies, wide-brimmed hats on their heads, rifles in buckets at their horses' sides.

This isn't much of an adventure, Harry told himself. A bird squawked in a bush nearby, and his chestnut horse jumped. It would be an adventure if Blaze was here, though. Oh pal, I hope nothing has happened to you.

* * *

On the fourth morning, the sergeant had new orders for Harry's Patrol.

'There's reports that the Boers may be moving some artillery into this area. You lads keep your eyes open for that. Report back if you see anything.'

They rode out, across the hard, dry ground, up the side of a stony hill. A huge, blue sky burned above them, with strange, black birds circling. The sun burned down. Horses and men dripped with sweat.

A flat plain stretched ahead, with more low hills in the distance. No sign of the enemy. Can't see anywhere that artillery could be hidden, thought Harry.

'Looks like the Boers have all run away,' one soldier called. Harry's chestnut jumped at the voice, and Harry hauled on its reins.

Suddenly, something happened to the ground in front of him. A blur, then a huge patch of earth lifted straight up into the air. Dirt and stones flew in all directions. Black smoke poured towards the sky.

COMING HOME

Boom! The sound battered at Harry's ears. At the same moment, another chunk of ground tore upwards. Boom! More stones flew. One smacked into Harry's side, and he gasped. More smoke billowed up.

His Army horse was bucking and screaming. Its head tossed madly. Its hooves flew in all directions. Terrified whinnies burst from its mouth. Harry fought to stay in the saddle.

'The Boers!' someone yelled. 'It's their artillery!'

Boom! Another explosion. Harry's steed leaped crazily. We've found the enemy after all, Harry thought. Or they've found us.

All around, the Patrol scattered. Men shouted at their horses, crouched low in their saddles as they fled the falling shells. Boom! The air was full of dust and smoke.

Harry hauled at the reins, tried to turn his horse around, but it was plunging and screaming so much, he could hardly control it.

Boom! The earth tore open just 20 yards away.

Hurtling stones and dirt thumped into Harry and his horse. The animal shrieked and bucked even more.

The Patrol was scattering in all directions, galloping back towards the hill they'd come over. Only Harry was still there, fighting to manage his mad steed.

Boom! Even closer. The earth exploded again. Harry's horse reared up on its hind legs. He gripped its mane and clung on.

Then he did what he'd never done to a horse before. He snatched his rifle, whacked the heavy barrel hard across the animal's back. The chestnut screamed again and began to gallop wildly after the rest of the Patrol.

Boom! But this shell burst well behind them. His horse was fleeing so fast that they were already catching up with the others. Harry crouched over the saddle.

'Well done, chum,' others in the Patrol told him, when they were all safely back on the far side of the hill. 'Thought that horse was going to throw you back there.'

'He was scared stiff,' Harry said. 'Not his fault. You don't know how any horse is going to behave in something like that.'

But while they trotted back to camp, and while they reported to their officer, who sent a messenger galloping off towards Base Camp, Harry kept thinking. He did know how one horse would behave. Please let that horse be all right.

He and others knelt in the trenches they'd dug all around the camp. The Boers might follow up their artillery attack with other forces. Nobody knew what might happen next.

Burning day turned into freezing dark. Men peered into the blackness, but nothing happened.

Harry thought of darkness in another land. A faraway land with green paddocks, stars above and a young horse safe in its barn. Wouldn't mind if I were there right now, he told himself.

* * *

The sun comes up. The sun goes down. Each night, Blaze finds a place to hide, in the trees or in a gulley where nobody can see him. Each day, he moves on. Those mountains, the barn and the pine tree: somehow his body and mind know where to go.

He is hungry all the time. He remembers the sweet grass of his master's farm. He can taste the apples and biscuits the young man would bring him before they rode out together.

Now he eats weeds and leaves. Sometimes he finds a patch of grass by a boulder or a tree and nibbles it down to the ground. He drinks from muddy puddles or streams.

He keeps watching for people. If he meets any, he knows he must run away. They might try to take him somewhere his master can't find him.

Late one afternoon, he passes near a farm. A small boy is playing out in a paddock. He looks up and sees Blaze. 'Horsey!' he calls. 'Here. Horsey!'

His voice sounds kind and happy. Blaze wants to go to him, to push his head against the boy's chest.

COMING HOME

But he hurries on. The small boy watches and keeps calling.

More days pass. Blaze makes his way down a gulley between steep hills. A noise grows in front of him. A rumbling, rushing sound. He sees the foaming river ahead.

He has crossed lots of rivers, but his master has always been there to guide him. He moves along the bank, trying to decide. He whinnies and snorts.

He can't see any crossing place. But he has to reach the far bank; he just knows it. He plunges into the chill water and starts to swim.

The river is fierce. It heaves at him, pulls him downstream. He fights to keep going, but he feels strangely weak. He tries to touch the bottom with his hooves, and his whole body goes under. He comes up, snorting with fear.

His legs struggle on. The bank seems miles away. The water keeps dragging at him.

At last, he feels something solid beneath his hooves. He comes staggering up onto the bank, slipping and almost falling. His lungs drag in air. His head droops down.

He stands there for a long time, panting and shivering. He wants to lie down and never move again, yet somehow he knows that he must.

Finally, he plods on. No matter how tired he is, no matter how many rivers or other dangers lie ahead, he will keep going.

The barn. The mountains. The paddocks. The young man. He sees them all in his mind. They are waiting for him. He mustn't let them down.

SEVEN

For another week, Harry rode out on patrols. His chestnut-coloured Army horse still shook and jerked at any strange sound. The Boer artillery shells seemed to have made him more nervous than ever.

There was no sign of any enemy. 'They're smart,' he heard a corporal saying. 'They know this land. They know how to hide and move.'

A letter reached Harry from home. His mother and father were well and sent him their love. They were sorry to hear about Blaze. Nobody had seen him.

'He is a wonderful brave horse,' Harry's mother

wrote. 'But anything could happen to him, dear son. You have to remember that.'

Harry knew what his mother meant. He knew, too, that when he returned home, he would search and search till he found his pal.

* * *

The days stayed burning hot. The nights stayed freezing cold. Food was poor, and some of the meat went rotten.

Men became sick and had to be taken back to Base Camp. Horses fell ill, too. Some died.

* * *

They'd eaten their breakfast of hard biscuits and stringy meat one morning. 'Patrol leaves in half an hour,' their sergeant called. 'Get ready.'

Harry strapped the saddle on his tired Army horse. The chestnut twitched and jittered.

Voices rose from the far end of camp; the sergeant hurried towards Harry and the others.

'A Boer train has been sighted. Our scouts think

it's carrying ammunition. You and other Patrols will ambush it. Check your rifles.'

They rode out a few minutes later, their officer leading. Not just one Patrol: 30 men, nearly half the Company.

They trotted across the stony plain, past the low, dry hills where more thorny bushes grew. Once again, Harry marvelled at how different this old, sun-baked land was from the green paddocks and bush back home. They crossed a riverbed with only a few muddy puddles. Harry's horse twitched at the water.

Two more miles on they crossed another dry riverbed. Something glittered ahead. The railway.

'Pile rocks on it!' the sergeant yelled. 'Rocks and branches. The train will have to stop!'

They dragged boulders across the ground and heaved them onto the track. They piled a log on top.

Their officer stared down the line. 'Hear that?'

A distant puffing was coming. The train.

'Take cover!' the officer called. 'Keep silent. When the train stops, wait for my signal.'

Quickly, they rode back into the dry riverbed, dismounted and stood by their horses, so they couldn't be seen above the banks. The puffing grew louder and nearer. They couldn't see the railway, but they heard iron wheels screech to a halt. Then silence.

'Give them a few minutes,' the officer said quietly. 'They'll get out to see what's happened. Then we'll attack. Stay silent.'

Harry's Army horse kept shifting and snorting. It whinnied. The officer glared. Harry patted the frightened animal's head, but it whinnied again.

'Take that horse further back, Private Barton!' the officer snapped.

Harry's face was red. He slid to the ground, took his horse's reins, began leading it further up the riverbed.

After 100 yards, he stopped and waited. No

sound. Minutes passed. He heard distant voices from the train.

The officer shouted once. Cheering burst out. Hooves pounded. Harry's side was attacking.

There was yelling from the train. A few shots rang out, and his horse jumped. A few more shots, then silence again.

Harry didn't know what to do. Finally, he mounted his horse and rode forward, rifle ready.

As he came up out of the riverbed, he saw the train, stopped in front of the boulders that blocked the track. Steam and smoke rose from its engine.

About 10 or 12 men stood near it. Their hands were raised in the air. Two lay on the ground. One held his leg, the other his arm.

Boers, Harry realised. The enemy. The Patrols surrounded them, rifles pointing. The officer was talking to one of the Boers. Slowly, the man took off the belt of bullets around his waist and dropped it on the ground.

Harry rode up and joined the others. He stared

at the enemy. Some had big, bushy beards. A couple were just young boys. They looked scared and skinny. Their clothes were ragged.

'You are now prisoners of war,' the officer was saying. 'You will be taken to a prison camp and treated fairly.'

The other soldiers were grinning. 'We showed them, pal,' Dick told Harry.

I didn't show them anything, thought Harry. He sighed, and patted his trembling horse. 'Not your fault. You tried.'

The Boers silently handed over their rifles and revolvers. Then they were put into the back of the train, with soldiers guarding them.

Other soldiers began unloading the ammunition. 'A nice gift for our side, lads!' the sergeant laughed. 'A good day for us.'

A good day for you blokes, Harry thought. *A real adventure for you. Ah, Blaze, if you were here, we'd have been part of it. I'm going to try and find you, but I wonder ... I wonder if we'll ever have any adventures again.*

* * *

Blaze has been in the bush for days.

He rushed into the trees after he came round a bend in a lonely track and saw two men riding towards him. They stopped their horses and called 'Hello, boy. Who are you?'

But Blaze didn't dare go near them. He couldn't go with anyone. They might take him anywhere.

So he galloped into the bush, ramming his way through shrubs and low branches. He didn't stop till he was far from the track, and green light was all around.

Now he can't find his way out. He doesn't dare move at night now. There are fallen trees to trip him, vines to tangle him, sudden drops and holes to injure him.

A branch has torn a deep cut along one side, when he fled from the two men. It hurts all the time. His master would spread cool cream over it and make it better. But not now.

His coat is filthy and muddy. His hooves are heavy with dirt. At home, his master would brush him till his coat shone. Here, there is nobody to make him clean and well. Nobody to make him less lonely.

And he is growing weaker. In the bush, there is hardly anything to eat. He nibbles on a few ferns, chews some soft bits of bark. When it rains, he licks water from leaves.

In the daytime, he wanders among the tall trunks, looking for a way out. His mind still sees the mountains, the barn and pine tree. He knows he must find them. His master will be there ... won't he?

One morning, the light seems brighter ahead. Blaze picks his way carefully among the trees, towards a yellow glare. Blue sky starts to show above.

Suddenly, he is out of the bush, standing on a slope of rough ferns and thorny bushes. A creek glitters below him.

He blinks in the sunlight. It hurts his eyes. Then

he starts moving down towards the water. He stops to pull at some ferns. They are tough and have no taste, but they will give him some strength.

He won't rest. He must go on. Out in the open, he seems to know the way more clearly, but he is getting weaker as each day passes. He must find his master before too long, or he may never find him at all.

EIGHT

Harry's nervous chestnut was taken away. 'You did your best, Private Barton,' the sergeant told him. 'But that one's no good for a fight. They'll use him for pulling wagons. You'll get another horse.'

Harry didn't care. No horse except Blaze would ever be the right one for him in this war. No horse except the one he might never see again. He had to face up to that, because another letter had arrived from his parents – another letter which said there had been no sign of his pal.

He and six other soldiers were ordered to take the Boers back to Base Camp.

They waited by the train all day. The prisoners

sat quietly. Harry heard the two young men singing softly. 'They're singing hymns!' said another soldier.

Harry stared. These men were the enemy, yet they looked and sounded just like ordinary people. How strange.

* * *

A wagon drawn by two horses arrived. The Boers climbed into it, along with Harry and another soldier, holding their rifles. The other troops rode beside them.

The journey to Base Camp took two days. They crossed another wide, stony plain, passed beside the first forest Harry had seen in South Africa. The days were still burning hot and followed by freezing nights, but Harry now knew to keep his greatcoat and blanket with him as soon as the sun went down.

On the second day, one of the older prisoners suddenly called out and pointed ahead. The soldiers gripped their rifles and stared. More enemy?

No. A dark cloud hung low in the sky. A cloud that was racing towards them. Harry felt his breath catch.

'Locust!' the Boer shouted. 'Cover face! Fast!'

Twenty seconds, and the storm of insects was on them. Millions of locusts, smacking into men and animals. They clung to faces, tangled in hair. Harry pressed one hand over his eyes.

'Horse!' another Boer called. 'Horse get fright!'

Harry jumped from the wagon, still covering his face. He could hardly see but he grabbed the leading horse and clung to its reins, pressing his hat over its eyes. The horde of insects swirled and clung. Someone was beside him, holding the other terrified steed.

Slowly, the locust swarm moved on. Harry blinked at the other man. It was one of the young Boers.

The boy smiled shyly and climbed back on the wagon. He could have escaped, Harry thought. But he helped us instead. Are these blokes really our enemy?

COMING HOME

* * *

They spent a couple of days at Base Camp, before a supply train took them back to the Front.

There was no Army horse for Harry when he returned. Instead, he began helping to build the blockhouse, the fort of wood and earth that was rising at one edge of their camp.

'The Boers are running out of food and supplies,' their sergeant said. 'They've started attacking some of our camps to steal things. We need to be ready.'

Slowly, the blockhouse grew. It was a strong, square shape, big enough to hold 30 men, with thick-timber walls. There were slits for rifles to fire through. Deep trenches stretched in front of the walls, on all four sides, where others could crouch and shoot.

'Those Boers will get a nasty surprise if they try anything here,' Ted grinned.

Harry said nothing. The war didn't feel like an adventure to him any more. He just wanted to get home.

Days passed. Their own supplies were getting low and on the bare plain there was hardly any wood for cooking fires. Men and animals were hungry. More horses began to fall sick.

One night, Harry was on sentry duty in the trenches with three other soldiers. They stared into the darkness. Above them, cold stars glittered. An icy wind breathed past.

Are you awake somewhere, Blaze? Harry wondered. *Or are you sleeping the very last sleep of all? I'm so sorry I had to leave you behind, old chum. If I could do things again, I wouldn't let that happen.* He tried to picture his horse, but it was getting harder. So many other things had happened.

After two hours, other soldiers came creeping out to take over sentry duty. They spoke in whispers, so no enemy could hear them. Harry returned to the blockhouse, wrapped his blanket around him, and lay down.

COMING HOME

He was cold but felt himself growing sleepy. He saw a barn and green paddocks. Pine trees and far-away mountains. Something moved by the barn. Could it be …

Men were talking near him. Silly fools. They were supposed to stay quiet, so no Boers could hear them. The sergeant would be angry.

Harry jerked awake. It wasn't talking. It was yelling. Yelling from the trenches outside. Other troops in the blockhouse were already jumping to their feet and grabbing for their rifles.

Their officer shouted orders. Harry jerked again at the next sound. *Blam! Blam! Blam!* Rifles blazed from the trenches. The Boers were attacking.

He threw his ammunition belt across his shoulders. He snatched his rifle and stumbled outside.

Flashes of fire came from all around. *Blam! Blam!* The enemy had surrounded them. More fire stabbed into the night as his own side shot back.

Harry raced for the nearest trench. Men were

throwing themselves down, and then blazing away into the darkness. From the blockhouse behind, one of their machine-guns burst out. *Blam-blam-blam-blam!*

Yells and cries filled the night. Harry stared ahead, trying to see. Suddenly, he glimpsed dark shapes rushing towards him, just 20 yards away.

He swung his rifle up and fired. *Blam!* The shot echoed in his ears. The shape seemed to fall. Had he hit someone? He ducked down in the trench, shaking and gasping.

Their machine-gun kept hammering. Men yelled and fired. Harry rose up again, rifle ready. His eyes searched for any attackers.

Go away, a voice inside his head begged. Go away. Don't make me shoot you. Something moved, only 10 yards in front. He whipped his rifle towards it.

Then an iron bar seemed to smash into his left

arm. At the same moment, another one crashed against the side of his head.

Harry began falling sideways. What had happened? Had the blockhouse fallen on him? Had an enemy hit him with a rifle butt?

He tried to get up, to struggle to his feet and keep fighting. He heard Ted's voice. 'Harry! Harry!'

But the dark night was getting darker. He felt himself sinking down again. The world vanished.

* * *

Steep hills rise in front of Blaze. He plods upwards, but every step feels so hard now.

His body keeps shaking. His hooves are heavy. His side throbs and burns where the tree branch tore into it, all those days or weeks ago.

He doesn't know how long it is since he ate properly. He has tried to look for grass. If ferns or shrubs are in front of him, he nibbles them, but it hurts to swallow.

His mouth is dry. He hasn't come across a stream

for a long time. The days have been so hot. He treads on, one step after another.

His head hangs down. Sometimes he stops, sways on his feet, tries to stare around him. Everything looks strange. He can't tell where he is.

Yet, somehow, he still knows where he must go. On towards the bright mountains and green paddocks. He has no idea how far away they are, or how long it will take, but on he goes.

His master will be worried about him. He must find his master, and then all will be well. But sometimes now, when his mind sees the barn and the pine tree beside it, his master isn't there any longer. What can this mean?

This morning the sun has gone. The day is cold, and dark rain has begun to pour from a black sky. Blaze shivers. His hooves slip as he climbs upwards.

The ground in front of him changes. He has reached the top of the hill. Ahead, a steep slope drops towards a river. At least he can drink now. Perhaps there will be grass to eat as well.

COMING HOME

His body keeps trembling. His eyes are blurry. He starts to move down the hill. It's hard to see where his hooves are treading.

He pushes through a group of low bushes. And suddenly the muddy ground gives way beneath him. He slips, plunges down into a ditch that the bushes had hidden.

A terrible pain tears through one leg. It collapses under him. Blaze flings back his head and screams.

Then he falls. Falls into darkness.

NINE

Harry felt wheels moving beneath him. Wheels that bumped and jerked. The Boers have captured me, he thought. I'm a prisoner.

He tried to move, but pain stabbed at his head, and all along his left arm.

Then he heard his mother's voice. 'Lie still, son. Lie still. You'll be all right.'

He must be home. Somehow the Army had got him back and he didn't even know it.

'Lie still.' His mother spoke again. 'You've had a bad time, soldier.'

It wasn't his mother. Harry forced his eyes open. A woman in a long, blue dress was looking down at him. She wore a white armband with a red cross on it. Harry started to understand.

'You're going to be all right,' the nurse said once more. 'You've got a badly broken arm: must have been a heavy bullet that hit you. And you'll have a fine scar on your forehead. All the girls will fuss over you.'

He could feel a wagon swaying beneath him. 'We're taking you to a hospital train,' the nurse told him. 'You and a few other boys who got hurt. You saved your fort, though. The Boers had to retreat. Your friends are safe. You rest now.'

My best friend, Harry tried to say. Where is ... ? But he felt his eyes close again.

* * *

The hospital train steamed slowly towards the coast. Big, red crosses were painted on its sides, but soldiers with rifles stood at each end of the carriage, eyes searching the dry, wide landscape.

Harry couldn't move his left arm. It throbbed

with pain. So did his head. When he touched it, he could feel a thick pad of bandages.

By the third day, he could sit up. The nurses fed him tea and soup. When he gazed around, he saw the four other soldiers from his Company. They smiled, spoke a few words to one another, but felt too exhausted to talk for long.

There was no sign of Ted or Dick. They must be all right, thank goodness.

That afternoon, as the train wound through a mountain pass, a doctor in a long, white coat came into the carriage.

'Well, Private Barton,' he told Harry. 'You've been in the wars, haven't you?'

Then the doctor laughed. 'What a silly thing for me to say! But you're going to be fine, lad. That arm is pretty smashed up. It will have to be in a sling for a long time. One of your friends saved you. He grabbed you and stopped the bleeding.'

Harry remembered Ted's voice calling to him. It

COMING HOME

must have been him. I have good human pals, too, he thought.

'You're going home.' The doctor smiled. 'A couple of weeks maybe till a ship arrives. Then you'll be off back to New Zealand. The Army's sent a telegram, telling your parents that you're coming. Don't worry – they know you're going to be all right.'

Harry lay back. His great adventure was over.

* * *

He spent 12 days at the Hospital Camp. Nurses took the bandages from his head. In the mirror, Harry saw a red scar from eyebrow to ear. He was lucky to be alive, he knew. More lucky than ... than someone else, perhaps.

His left arm kept throbbing with pain. Thick bandages and a sling held it still.

After three days, he was allowed out of bed. After a week, he could walk slowly around. He passed a ward with armed soldiers at the door. Wounded Boer prisoners were inside. *I hope they'll be all right,* Harry thought.

Another couple of days, and he began helping with the horses that pulled supply or hospital wagons. With his good arm, he brought them water, brushed them and talked to them. One of them pushed his head against Harry's chest, and the young man hugged him for a second.

A telegram came from his mother and father. DEAR SON. LOVE YOU. HOPE SEE YOU SOON. TAKE ALL CARE.

The telegram said nothing about Blaze. Harry knew what this meant. His horse was gone forever. He lay somewhere in the bush, or beside a river.

He would have been brave till the end, Harry told himself. I know he would have been. And he was the strongest, most beautiful horse in the world. I'll spend the rest of my life remembering him.

Another three days, and a ship arrived. A wagon took Harry down to the wharf. Another soldier from his Company, who had been shot in the leg, was with him.

'I can't wait to be back home,' the other young

man grinned. 'Be so good to see everyone again!' Harry tried to smile, too, but he knew that there was someone at home he wouldn't see again.

They watched men in khaki uniforms coming down the gangway. The new soldiers looked fit and excited.

Horses were being lifted in nets from the ship. Most squealed and kicked as they were lowered. Only one stayed calm and quiet.

As it stood tall on the wharf, and the net was pulled away, Harry saw a glossy, brown coat. His breath stopped. It couldn't be. It ...

The horse tossed its head, and snorted. A dark head with no white patch. Harry sighed, and turned away.

Finally, the wounded men moved slowly up the gangway. Some leaned on sticks. Many had bandages on arms or heads.

Navy officers saluted them as they reached the deck. 'Well done, lads. New Zealand is proud of you. You're on your way home.'

Harry felt weak and worn out. But he stood to attention and returned the salutes.

*　*　*

Blaze staggers along beside a river. There seem to be still more hills in front of him. It's hard to lift his head now, so he can't be sure.

Every time his injured leg touches the ground, agony tears through his whole body. He limps on for a few minutes, stands with his leg off the ground till the worst pain has gone, then moves onwards.

Every day he feels weaker, and moves more slowly. He tries to eat, but it gives him no strength.

He comes to some swampy ground and starts to cross. He sinks up to his knees. When he tries to pull himself free, he nearly falls.

Terror floods through him. He will die here, and never reach his home. He heaves himself free, staggers to firm ground. He stands there for hours, shivering and panting. The wound in his side throbs and burns. Finally, he stumbles on.

The river leads him down to a plain. It isn't far

away, but the sun goes down and comes up twice before he reaches it. Through the nights, he stays still. His whole body trembles and aches.

On the day he finally reaches the plain, clouds begin to fill the sky. He lifts his head, and feels dizzy. Far away, he sees something high. Something blue and white. Mountains.

He seems to know them. Can they be ... ? The barn is there in his mind. So are the pine trees and the paddocks. The young man? He can't tell.

He begins to limp onwards. He can't. His legs give way, and he sinks to the earth. He tries to rise, but his body won't obey him.

This is the end. He can't go any further. He will never see his master again.

TEN

It was three weeks till the hospital ship reached Wellington. Harry's left arm was still in a sling.

People on the wharf clapped as the wounded men came down the gangway. They gave flowers and chocolate to the soldiers. 'You're heroes, lads!' they called. 'Real heroes!'

Harry didn't feel like a hero. He just felt tired and sad. And lonely.

He had to spend another week at Base Camp in Wellington, while doctors checked that his arm was getting better. Soldiers training to go to South Africa asked him what it was like. 'Look after your pals,' Harry told them.

A letter came from his parents. 'We can't wait

COMING HOME

for you to be home, dear son. Nobody has seen any sign of Blaze. There are so many dangerous rivers and gulleys. Even the strongest horse can vanish and never be seen again. We're so sorry.'

After he read the letter, Harry walked to the edge of the camp by himself. For a long time, he stood and gazed at the faraway green hills

* * *

A train took him back home. He remembered that first train, months ago. He and Ted and Dick and their horses. All of them so excited at the great adventure ahead.

He hoped Dick and Ted would come home safely. He'd write to them. His other pal ... Harry knew there'd never be a horse like him again.

His parents were waiting for him by the little station shed. His mother burst into tears and kissed him, while his father shook his good hand over and over again.

They drove back to the farm in their little wagon, behind a slow, old farm horse. The paddocks were fresh and green – so different from that rocky, sun-burned land of the last few weeks. Sheep and cows watched them pass.

'Blaze?' Harry asked, just once.

His mother held her son's good hand. 'I'm sorry, Harry,' she said. 'I'm sorry.'

I'll look for you when I'm well again, Harry promised himself. I will, old pal. I'll find where you lie, and I'll remember you forever.

* * *

A week passed. Each day, Harry felt a little stronger. Each day, he walked around the farm.

He stood by the barn and gazed at the paddocks where he would talk to Blaze every morning. He touched the fence rail where he used to hang his pal's saddle.

'I suppose I'd better think about getting another horse,' he said one day at breakfast.

His father nodded. 'There's a cattle and horse sale on Ted's family farm next Friday. We can go there if you like, son.'

COMING HOME

Harry's mother said nothing. But when her son stood up from the table, she stood, too, and kissed him again.

Outside, Harry walked slowly towards the barn. Another few days and he should be able to take off the sling. It was time to start helping his father again. Time to forget what he'd lost.

He stood by the pine tree and gazed around once more. The barn, the paddocks, the distant mountains – all these places that he and his wonderful friend had known together.

Harry sighed. He'd better go and talk to his father about a new horse.

A faint noise came from behind him.

* * *

Somehow, Blaze is stumbling forward again. He's dragged himself to his feet, and plods on. But he understands that if he falls again, it will be for the last time.

Even putting one hoof in front of another is agony

now. Shudders shake his body. His injured leg and torn side are endless throbs of pain.

He's too weak even to crop the rough grass. Rain falls on him, and cold winds blast at him. He staggers on, one step after another.

He must be getting closer to those mountains. But it's hard for him to lift his head and look. When he tries, everything seems blurry.

This morning, the sun is low. He's on flat ground, with green grass. Birds call from nearby.

Blaze manages to gaze around. He sees trees, and fences with wooden rails. He starts to limp on again. Then he stops.

He seems to know those wooden rails. He takes a step, and his injured leg sends pain stabbing through him.

But he takes another step. And another. There is a building ahead, and he seems to know that, too.

His heart beats faster. He comes around the corner of the building, and stops again, the sun dazzling his tired eyes.

Something stands in front of him. A shape. A man, facing away from him.

Blaze hears himself breathe out. The shape turns.

* * *

Harry's parents were still finishing breakfast when they heard their son begin to shout. They stared at each other.

The shouting grew louder. Harry was crying out.

'He's fallen and hurt himself!' the young man's mother gasped. 'Hurry!'

They rushed out towards the barn, where their son kept shouting. Not just shouting, but laughing and cheering, too. And another voice was there. A voice they knew, somehow.

They hurried around the corner. Then they stopped and stared.

Their son stood there. His left arm was in its sling. His right arm was around the neck of a horse.

The horse was hurt. One leg was off the ground, and a gash showed on its skinny side. It was covered with mud and dirt so they could hardly see what colour it was.

But its head was pushed against Harry's chest, while it kept whinnying softly to him. Their son laughed as he held it. Laughed and cried at the same time.

He saw his parents and called to them. 'Look! Look!'

The horse moved, and a white patch showed on its forehead.

'It's Blaze!' the young man exclaimed. 'Blaze has come home!'

Harry's mother smiled. 'You both have. You've both come home.'

* * *

Blaze's body keeps shaking. His wounds throb. He's weak and dizzy.

It doesn't matter. He's found his master. All the pain, all the tiredness – they're nothing, now that his master's arm is around him. Everything will be all right.

COMING HOME

He hears Harry talking. He doesn't understand the words. He never has. But he understands their meaning, and they fill his heart with joy.

* * *

'Blaze! Blaze, my dearest, bravest pal! We're together again. And we're never going to be apart now, as long as we live!'

The South African War, 1899-1902, was fought between soldiers from the British Empire and Dutch settlers called Boers. South Africa at that time was a British colony, but many of its farmers were Dutch, and wanted more independence.

Fighting began, and volunteers from Canada, Australia and New Zealand came to fight on the British side. Many of them were skilled horsemen who could ride and fight in dangerous places.

This book is the story of one young rider and his precious horse.

I Wish

ONE

Trent Karam was bored.

He and his mum had moved to this grotty flat in a different town. They'd been here two days, and Trent was totally bored.

His computer hadn't arrived. There weren't any other kids in the street. One skinny guy who looked about Trent's age had gone past and stared at him. Trent stared back.

Somewhere down the hill was the school he would be starting at tomorrow. How long till the kids there found out how ordinary and boring he was?

* * *

'Trent?' His mother was calling. 'Do you know what these are?'

In the living room, Mrs Karam stood staring into a cardboard carton full of books. 'Are these yours? I don't recognise them.' Trent stared at the strange covers. 'Not mine.'

His mother sighed. 'The moving people must have got someone else's stuff mixed up with ours.' Trent picked up one of the books. *Take It Slowly*, by ... somebody. He read a couple of pages. Boring.

His mother glanced at her watch. 'Oh no, I'll be late! I have to write an article about the new hospital.' She grabbed her car keys and headed to the door. 'Could you sort this stuff out, please, love? Make yourself a sandwich for lunch.'

The car spluttered off up the drive. Trent picked up another book from the strange carton. *Works Naturally*, by ... somebody else. Totally boring. Suddenly, he felt wild at everything. At moving to this boring new town, and this grotty flat, and his missing computer, and these boring books, and ... and *everything!*

He drew his arm back and chucked *Works Naturally* across the living room.

The book flew through the air and whacked into the far wall before landing on the floor, pages open.

Then the book spoke. 'Ow!' it said. 'Ya idiot! That hurt!'

TWO

Trent stared at the book lying on the floor. 'Wha – what?'

'I said that hurt!' the book told him. 'Ya dumb-bum! Would you like *me* to chuck *you* against a wall?'

'I ... you ... no, sorry,' Trent mumbled. This must be a dream. Or maybe a nightmare. No, a daymare. He'd better make sure he was really awake. He pinched his side to check. 'Ouch!' he yelped. 'Good!' went the book. 'You deserve a bit of pain.'

Trent swallowed. 'Can you see me?'

'Of course I can see you!' the book's voice was high and squeaky. 'And you're seriously ugly. Pick me up!'

Very carefully, Trent moved forward and lifted *Works Naturally* from the floor. It had fallen open at a page with an illustration. A little green figure, looking at him.

The green figure moved. *'Aaaarghhh!'* yelled Trent, and dropped the book.

'Ow! Ya idiot!' it shouted. 'What are ya doin'?'

Very carefully, Trent picked up the book once more. The illustration moved again. The green figure was lifting its green head from the page. 'Whoaaa!' Trent shouted, and dropped the book a second time.

Works Naturally whacked onto the carpet again. 'No! Ahh!' the voice yelled. 'Ya dozy moron! Pick me up!'

Trent picked up the book, placed it on the table, opened it, and jumped back.

The tiny figure on the page glared up at him. It was all green – hair, face, legs, hands, shorts, teeshirt. It stretched two green arms, shook a green head, and sat half up on the page.

'Took your time, didn't ya?'

Trent swallowed. 'Wh ... What are you?'

'I'm sore! Some brainless human keeps dropping me!' The creature's green teeshirt had words on it, also in green. FAIRIES SUCK, they read.

'What are you?' Trent asked again.

There was a green stud in the green nose. The green hair was cut in a mohawk on the green skull.

'I'm a book-elf, of course. Man, you're thick!'

Trent wasn't sure he'd heard properly. 'A book-shelf?'

'A book-*elf*!' the creature shrieked.

'Is that like a genie?'

The book-elf looked pleased. 'A genius? Yes, I'm a genius, all right.'

Trent shook his head. 'No, I mean ... ' he stopped. A car was spluttering down the driveway. His mother.

Trent shoved the green head back inside the covers. The green hair felt dry and bristly. He closed the book hard. *'Aarrghhh!'* a voice went. 'Ya stup ... '

I WISH

Trent whipped *Works Naturally* back into the carton of strange books.

'The hospital had everything ready for me,' Mrs Karam said. 'Who were you talking to, love?'

'Um ... myself,' Trent said.

His mum laughed. 'Anything interesting in that carton of books?'

'Interesting?' Trent shrugged. 'Yeah ... could be.'

* * *

They carried on unpacking through the afternoon. 'Drove past your new school on the way home,' Trent's mum said. 'Looks nice.'

Nice till the kids there found out how ordinary he was. But Trent wasn't thinking about his new school. He kept glancing at the carton of books. Had it really happened? Maybe he'd better pinch himself to make sure. No, there was the bruise from the first pinch. 'We'll have to send those books back to whoever owns them.' Trent jerked at his mother's words. Had he just heard a faint voice yelling, 'Another thick-brained human!'?

'Early night, eh, love?' Mrs Karam yawned. 'Maybe your computer will arrive tomorrow.'

His computer. Trent had almost forgotten it.

Half an hour later, he and his mother were in bed. Half an hour after that, Trent tiptoed through to the living room, and opened the carton of books.

THREE

Which book had the bookshelf – the book-elf – been in? *Just Write*? No, the one underneath. *Works Naturally.* There was a noise coming from inside it. Someone moaning. He must have hurt the weird midget when he shut the book.

Then Trent grinned. It wasn't someone moaning. It was someone snoring.

* * *

The pages opened to show a green figure lying on its back with its mouth open. Every time the figure snored, its green mohawk shook.

Trent poked the book-elf's shoulder. A green mouth snapped shut. Two green eyes snapped open. 'It wasn't me!' gabbled the book-elf. 'I didn't do anything!'

'Shhhh!' hissed Trent. The green face glared. 'Don't you shhhh me, ya dimwitted – '

'You'll wake my mum!' warned Trent. The book-elf kept glaring but went quiet.

'What's your name?' Trent asked.

Green shoulders shrugged. 'I don't bother with a name. I'm too special. You can call me "Your Highness". Or "Genius", like you did before.'

Trent grinned again. 'I'll call you Gene. So, what *is* a book-elf?'

Gene sighed. 'Man, you're dumb! Book-elves are like the spirits of stories. We move from book to book and make sure they really grab readers.'

'If you can move from book to book, how come you're stuck in this one?' The book-elf scowled. 'Slob.' Trent scowled straight back. 'Don't you call me a slob!'

'No, I mean SLOB – Scary Lords Of Book-elves. They're my bosses. They stuck me in here because they said I was rude to people. The bone brains!'

Trent grinned a third time. 'Rude to people? You? Never!'

Gene nodded. 'Unbelievable, eh? But the SLOB slobs stuffed me in here till I do better.'

'Are you a real genie?' Trent asked. 'Can you grant wishes and stuff?'

The book-elf hesitated. 'Sort of.'

'What d'you mean – "sort of"?'

'Trent?' Mrs Karam's voice came from her bedroom. 'What are you doing?'

'I ... I'm getting a drink of water. Just asking the glass where it was.'

His mother laughed sleepily. 'You funny kid. Good night.'

'Night, Mum.' Trent realised he'd shut *Works Naturally* again. He put it back in its carton, went back to bed, and couldn't sleep.

* * *

His new school was called North Valley and his new teacher was Mr Masoe.

After lunch, Mr Masoe started reading to Room 21. Trent looked around the class.

A dark-haired guy drawing in his folder looked sort of familiar. Across the row sat a girl with fair hair. Next to her was a guy with braces.

Then Trent stared. The book his new teacher was reading – it sounded like that one from the carton. *Take It Slowly.*

Mr Masoe grinned at Room 21. 'I'm reading you this because we're visiting The Indoor Adventure Centre tomorrow, remember? We're going on the climbing wall.'

Kids made pretend-scared faces at one another. None of them looked at Trent. He hadn't expected them to. He was ordinary. If only he could do something special. Yeah, like what?

His first day at North Valley finally ended. As he followed the other kids out of Room 21, Trent realised something. The dark-haired folder-drawer was the guy who'd wandered past the flat yesterday.

I WISH

He realised something else, too. He had a major question to ask Gene the book-elf.

FOUR

Mrs Karam was in the living room. 'Hello, love. How was the first day?' Trent muttered something.

'Your computer arrived,' his mum said. 'The movers found it in their truck.'

Trent twitched. 'Where's those books?'

Mrs Karam laughed. 'Still here. The moving company don't know anything about them. We'll give them to a Gala Day sometime. I'll move them out of the way as soon as we've got a bit more sorted.'

His mother went into the kitchen. Trent opened the carton, and took out *Take It Slowly*. He put his ear close to *Works Naturally*. Silence. He left the second book in the carton, and took the other to his room. By dinner time, he was nearly halfway through. It wasn't boring after all. It was cool. There were accidents, dangers, rock climbing, disasters.

* * *

Later, after his mother was asleep, Trent crept through to the living room holding *Take It Slowly.*

He lifted *Works Naturally* from its carton and opened it.

'Had a good day?' the green face grunted. 'I've had a boring day.'

Trent stared at the green teeshirt. The words on it read DWARFS ARE SHORT – OF A BRAIN.

'You've changed your teeshirt,' he said.

'Don't you?' the book-elf snapped. 'Are you smelly as well as stupid?'

Trent ignored him. 'You say those SLOB dudes put you in here. What do you have to do to get out?'

Gene sniffed. 'I have to help people, and stop being rude to them. How unfair is that?'

'And you *can* grant wishes?'

Gene hesitated again. 'They can only be wishes

from books. I'm a *book*-elf, right? And ... No, forget it.'

Trent picked up *Take It Slowly.* 'This book. It – '

The book-elf sighed. 'Hold it in front of my nose, ya thickie. *Pleeeez!*'

Trent held the book so it almost touched the tiny green nose with its tiny green stud. Gene breathed in deeply.

'Okay,' said the squeaky voice. 'It's about these high school kids who go tramping in the bush. They get caught in a storm. A flood nearly kills one girl. One guy climbs a cliff, and – '

'How do you know all that?' demanded Trent.

Gene grinned a green grin. 'I'm a book-elf, remember?'

Trent swallowed. 'Our teacher's taking us to the climbing wall at The Indoor Adventure Centre. If you make me a brilliant climber, like the guy in the book, then you'll really help me, and SLOB will be pleased. Right?'

Gene nodded. 'You got a deal. Ummmm ... it won't take you long, will it? The climbing?'

'A few minutes, I suppose. Why?'

'Trent?' Just like the night before, his mother's voice made Trent jerk *Works Naturally* shut. A muffled yelp came from inside.

'Are you talking to the glass again?' his mother asked.

'No, I'm talking to the water.'

His mother was silent. Then – 'Are you feeling sick, love?'

'No, I'm okay.' *Works Naturally* went back into the carton and Trent headed back to his room. He didn't sleep well that night, either.

FIVE

The climbing wall was amazing, Mr Masoe said on the bus next morning.

The skinny guy was two seats in front, drawing in another folder. He didn't say anything to anyone but the girl with the fair hair said something to everyone. Her name was Deena. Trent knew this, because other kids kept going, 'Shut up, Deena!'

Inside the Centre, the climbing wall towered above them, like the cliff in *Take It Slowly*. Trent remembered his wish and swallowed.

A fit-looking woman appeared and smiled at the class. 'Hello, people.'

She showed them a leather belt, hanging from

wires. 'This is a harness. If you need to let go, the harness holds you. You can't fall – I'll be holding the rope. Plus you wear a helmet in case you headbutt our expensive wall.'

The instructor (Katie, Mr Masoe called her) showed how it was done. 'Push with your legs,' she said, as she moved smoothly up. 'Get your whole hand on each grip. Don't look down.' That was all in *Take It Slowly*, too, Trent remembered.

'So?' Katie asked. 'Who's going first?'

'You, Richie?' Their teacher nodded to a stocky guy, who put on the harness and helmet, and climbed up about five metres. Then one foot slipped, and he skidded back down till the harness held him. Room 21 clapped.

'Deena?' said Mr M. The fair-haired girl talked to the wall as she puffed up. Then she yelled, 'Rock climbing really rocks, eh?' Room 21 groaned.

'Kieran?' It was the silent, dark-haired boy. He pulled himself from ledge to rock till he was over halfway up, then swung back down in big leaps while Katie played out the rope. He's good, Trent realised. But I'll be better. I have to be special. Please, Gene?

'Who's next?' Trent must have moved because the teacher's eyes met his. 'You, Trent?'

Suddenly, Trent's mouth spoke. 'Okay. I've done some climbing.' He hadn't meant to say those words. He felt his stomach start to churn.

As he stepped forward, a tingling grew in his arms and hands. It rushed down into his legs. Power poured through him. His wish was working!

'Take your time,' Katie told him.

Trent looked upwards. Then he began to climb – brilliantly.

* * *

It was like magic. His body flowed up the wall. His legs pushed. His arms reached. His hands gripped.

'Well, well!' went Katie, already way below him. 'A mountaineer!' Trent snaked on. He was halfway up already. He was being so special!

I WISH

'Tricky bit ahead,' he heard Katie call. 'Take it slowly.'

Take it slowly. The title of that book: how weird. But he didn't need to take it slowly. His wish was working perfectly. Trent gazed upward. A rock jutted above him. He could reach it easily. He bent his legs and flung himself up.

All the power and strength vanished from his body. He missed the rock and fell.

SIX

'Help!' he squealed. He thudded into the wall, helmet first. 'Owwww!' he yelled. 'Oooo!'

Kids started to laugh. Trent heard some going, 'Oooo!' and others pretending to squeal, 'Help!'

He clung to the wall. What had happened? What had gone wrong?

The harness and rope supported him as he came swinging down. 'You Okay?' Katie asked. 'Got a bit carried away, eh?'

Trent stared at the floor. Why had his wish ended so suddenly? Had something happened to Gene?

He half watched the others climb. Nobody got as high as him, but then nobody else made an idiot of themselves like him, either.

*   *   *

Back in school, they read plays by themselves. 'You're going to act them in your groups next week,' Mr Masoe announced. 'Start choosing one.'

Trent looked at one about a guy's bedroom that was so messy, even his dog wouldn't go in. Another with a guy feeling nervous about playing the guitar in a school concert.

After that, Mr M. read them more of *Take It Slowly,* 'now that you know what it's like'. He didn't look at Trent.

Trent's head kept fizzing with questions. Why had his wish ended like that? Why had he fallen from the wall? Should he throw useless Gene over a wall, too?

*   *   *

As he walked uphill towards the flat, he saw skinny Kieran ahead of him. The other boy saw Trent and slowed down, then kept going. Huh, thought Trent, who'd want to walk with someone as useless as me?

A note from his mother was on the table. *Out*

researching article on meteors. Had a good day?'

No, I've had a stink day, Trent thought. And someone else is going to have an even stinkier day.

From the carton, he lifted out *Take It Slowly*. Underneath it was one called *Duo*. Its cover showed a guy playing a guitar. He picked up *Works Naturally*. Snoring started inside. Snoring that was too loud to be real.

The book-elf lay on his back, eyes shut. 'Wake up!' Trent shook the book. The green eyes shut tighter. Trent shook harder.

Today, Gene's green teeshirt read, TROLLS PLAY WITH DOLLS. His green eyelids opened. 'Oh, it's you. Ummm ... everything go all right?'

'Yeah, it did.'

The book-elf looked pleased. 'It did? Cool. Told you I was a genius. SLOB will be pleased.'

'It went all right – till it stopped. How come my wish ended so suddenly?'

Gene stared at his green toes. 'If a book-elf

doesn't behave like the stupid SLOB rules say we should, then our spells don't work as long.'

He gave a cheesy grin. 'Still, I tried. My next one should last longer.'

Trent stared. 'So, if I ask for another wish, can you do it?'

'Not yet,' the book-elf muttered. 'I need time to charge my batteries.'

Trent blinked. 'Batteries?'

The green figure sighed. 'Humans are dumb, but you're the dumbest. Doing wishes is hard work. I need to build up my energy. Come back in a couple of days. Read a book while you're waiting; it might give you a few clues.'

'What book?' Trent asked.

The book-elf sighed again. '*Any* book!' He waved a hand at the carton. 'They're books, in case ya were too thick to ... in case ya hadn't noticed.'

Trent picked *Duo*, with its guitar guy. He read it till his mum came home. He read it after dinner and in bed. By the time he put his light out, he had a new plan.

SEVEN

On Wednesday, at breakfast, Mrs Karam told Trent about the meteor article a magazine wanted her to write. 'I'm going to see an artist who paints stars and galaxies and stuff. Sounds cool.'

Trent just grunted.

He read more of *Duo* before he left for school and decided the guitar stuff was quite interesting. He knew about climbing *and* guitars now. Pity he couldn't do either of those things. Or could he ... ?

* * *

'Would you like to hear more of *Take It Slowly*?' Mr Masoe asked at school. Room 21 went 'Oh, yeah!'

'Then you have to prove you've been listening.

We'll have a test on what I've read.' Room 21 went 'Oh, no!'

There were 12 questions. Trent knew nearly all of them. He'd heard the book in class; read the book at home; thought about the book everywhere.

'Swap answers with someone,' went Mr M. Deena flapped hers at Trent.

He stared at what the girl had written. *No. 1: Don't know ... No. 2: Haven't a Clue ... No. 3: Don't ask me ... No. 4: Wasn't listening.*

'Anyone get them all right?' asked their teacher. Deena pointed. 'He did – Trent.'

Mr Masoe said, 'Good stuff, Trent. A point for the Cougars.'

'Yay!' cheered Deena and some others. Trent suddenly understood what the names and numbers on the whiteboard meant. *Cougars, Wildcats, Wolverines, Panthers ... Fluffybums??*

So, Wednesday at school was okay. Ordinary, but okay. Trent plodded uphill towards the flat, working out his next wish in his mind.

* * *

Could he tell his mum about his wishes? And about Gene? No, she'd want to see the book-elf. And she'd want to find the books' real owner.

All through the evening, while he read more of *Duo*, he kept glancing at the carton that his mum had tucked away beside their old couch..

He'd wait till his mum was asleep – till her light went out. Then in another half hour he'd get up and check on Gene.

In bed, he glanced at his clock. 9.22 pm.

A few minutes later, his eyes twitched open. He'd nearly fallen asleep! The light in the living room was still on. It was only ... he stared at his clock. It was 7.14 am on Thursday.

* * *

As he came out onto the footpath, Kieran went past. The two boys looked at each other. There was more play reading before lunch. 'Okay, now get in your groups and choose one play,' Mr Masoe said. 'You'll act it for the whole class next week. Yes, with props and costumes, if you want.'

There were five other Cougars: Deena; Conrad (the guy with braces); the other guy Richie; a tall girl and a small girl.

'Let's do the one about the guy and the concert and the guitar,' Deena said.

Conrad shook his head. 'Let's do the one about the concert and the guitar and the guy.'

'All right,' went Richie. 'Sweet,' went the tall girl. 'No worries,' went the small girl. They all looked at Trent.

'Nah,' he said. 'Let's do the one about the guitar and the guy and the concert.' The others laughed.

He felt good. Maybe he didn't need to rely on wishes and Gene after all. He could just –

Right then, his mouth spoke. 'Actually, I play the guitar quite a bit.'

* * *

Why did he say that? Trent tried to understand as he walked home. He'd never played a guitar in his life!

Once again, his mother wasn't home. Trent headed for the carton of books and lifted out *Works Naturally*. He had to ask the book-elf what was happening.

He turned the pages. 'Hey, Gene – ' he began.

The small green figure lay on its side, one green cheek resting on a green hand. Today, his teeshirt read VAMPIRES *REALLY* SUCK.

'Ge ... ' Trent started again. Then he stopped. The book-elf's eyes were really shut. Its body lay still. It seemed different, somehow. Different and far away.

Trent closed the book softly and put it back in the carton.

EIGHT

Friday. Room 21 played soccer before interval. 'The running's good for you,' Mr Masoe grinned as they puffed and panted. 'It's our cross-country in a couple of weeks.'

After interval, they began planning their plays. 'You be the guitarist,' Deena told Trent, and his stomach lurched sideways. 'Can you bring a guitar?'

'I left it behind when we moved house,' he mumbled. Conrad and Richie, and the tall girl (Briar) and the small girl (Baillee) all looked at him. Deena was too busy giving orders to notice.

'We don't need much scenery and stuff,' she announced. 'A few chairs – and someone's gotta get a guitar for Trent.'

Trent's stomach lurched sideways and downwards. 'I ... I can just pretend.'

But as he walked home that afternoon, he made his mind up. He was going to tell Gene his next wish.

* * *

Trent carefully opened *Works Naturally*. Was the book-elf still aslee ...

'BOO!' The yell made him jump a metre in the air. Gene was sitting up on the page, smirking. His green teeshirt showed a troll dropping a warty-faced small creature into its mouth, over the words GOBLIN GOBBLIN.

'Give you a fright?' The book-elf sneered. 'Man, you humans are wimps. Waddaya want?'

Trent thought of his plan. 'This book – *Duo* ... '

A small, green finger pointed to a small, green nose. 'Put it here, remember?'

Trent put it there. He stared while the book-elf breathed in. 'Okay,' went Gene. 'So, this guitar guy's band has gone down the tubes, but then he joins up with this girl singer, and there's lots of kissy-kissy, spewy-spewy stuff.'

Trent stared again. 'How *do* you do that?'

The book-elf grinned. '*You* have to turn the pages, but *we* just go straight through them.'

'I see,' went Trent, who didn't really see at all. 'Well, my next wish is to play the guitar like the guy in that book.'

The green mohawk nodded. 'No worries.'

'Sure?' Trent asked. 'It won't finish too short, like last time? SLAB or SLOP won't mess it up?'

'SLOB!' the book-elf shrieked. 'Ya ignorant – Look, you'll be fine, as long as you don't – '

But Trent was still thinking. 'There's another thing, too.'

'There's *always* another thing!' protested the small shape. 'You're a pain!'

'And you're rude! You're not allowed to be rude, remember? Not if you ever want to get out of this book.'

The green throat swallowed. 'Ummm ... I forgot. Ummm ... thank you, oh clever and handsome young human.'

Trent tried not to laugh. 'Tell me why my mouth keeps sounding off. Why does it say I'm cool, when ... when I'm not.'

The book-elf muttered, 'If SLOB think you don't deserve the wish, they can stuff things up for you in all sorts of ways. That's probably it.'

He gave a yawn that Trent felt sure was fake. 'Now, I need to do more recharging. I've got a busy time ahead.'

NINE

It rained nearly all weekend. His mother was busy writing her article about the Science Artist. 'He does these brilliant paintings of planets and stars. He's called Brad and his son goes to your school.'

Trent felt bored and ordinary. He still didn't know anybody around here to hang out with, so he started another book from the carton. It was called *Out of Time,* about a lonely kid who went for long runs along the roads near his town. Then one day a huge tornado struck, and he seemed to be hurled into another universe.

He also thought about his second wish. The wish that would turn him into a brilliant guitarist for the play and make him so cool and special. It had to.

Just before tea, Mrs Karam announced, 'I've got to shoot down to the supermarket. Want to come, love?'

Trent shook his head. The moment he heard the car splutter off, he hurried to the carton of books.

He pulled out *Works Naturally,* and started to open it. Instantly, a voice squealed. 'Push off!'

Trent stopped. 'I know it's you,' the voice went on. 'Look, your wish is gonna work. I need some quiet time, so push off – *pleeez*!'

* * *

On Monday morning, Trent had just reached the bottom of the hill when skinny Kieran came out of the corner dairy. His bag was covered with a painting of a galaxy, a glittering wheel of stars.

'Hey,' went Trent. The other boy muttered something back.

They walked on together. 'Cool bag.' Trent pointed to the galaxy painting, packed with silver and orange stars.

'My Dad did it. He does illustrations and stuff for magazines.'

Trent stared. He remembered his mum. 'Hey, is he the one who – '

But a voice was yelling from the far side of the road.

'Trent!' went Deena. 'Hey, Trent, we've found you a guitar!'

* * *

They rehearsed their plays after lunch. Deena bossed everyone around as usual. 'Trent's the guitarist; I'll be D J Kool; Conrad, you be the useless organiser; Richie and Briar and Baillee, you be ...

'Oh,' she added. 'And we have a guitar. We can borrow one from the Music Room. Not till tomorrow, though.'

Suddenly Trent heard his mouth start up. 'Shouldn't be a problem. As long as I can have a couple of minutes to tune it.'

He squeezed his lips shut so fast that his teeth

clicked. Were SLOB trying to make him look a ... a slob?

The Panthers were doing a play about a canoe. The Wildcats and Wolverines (Kieran sat among his group, drawing again. Was he an artist, too?) were acting stories about a skateboard contest and a weird scientist. The Fluffybums were zombies.

'Last rehearsal tomorrow morning,' Mr Masoe told them. 'Then you perform the plays after lunch in the hall.'

'Points for our groups, Mr M.?' called Deena – of course.

Their teacher nodded. 'Remember you can use props and stuff, if you want. I hear we're going to have a proper guitar for our gun guitarist?' Trent gazed at the floor. *This wish has to work*, he told himself for the trillionth time. *It just has to.*

TEN

At home, Trent headed straight for the carton of books, and opened *Works Naturally*.

The book-elf jerked. 'Can't you knock? I might be changing my teeshirt or something!'

Today's one showed the warty-faced creature in a big cooking pot of water on a fire, with the words GOBLIN BUBBLIN.

But Trent wasn't interested. 'You're sure it's going to be okay?' he asked. 'The guitar-playing? Tomorrow?'

The green mohawk nodded. 'No sorrow about tomorrow.'

Trent heard his mother's car spluttering up the

drive. He spoke again, quickly. 'No problems with PLOP?'

'SLOB!' squeaked the book-elf. 'Look – just – '

Just what? But the front door was opening. Trent closed the book fast, as a voice yelped, 'Careful, ya stu –' He dropped it back in the carton as his mother appeared.

'Who were you talking to, love?'

'Errrr ... myself.' As his mum gazed at him, Trent added, 'Just practising my lines for the class play.'

* * *

'I've been doing another interview with Brad,' Trent's mother said at dinner. 'He's working on this big painting of a supernova – an exploding star. It's amazing.'

'His son's in my class,' Trent told her. 'He's okay.'

But Trent's mind wasn't on Kieran. It was on the guitar he was meant to play tomorrow in front of Room 21. The guitar that was going to shame him totally unless Gene did his job. The job he *had* to do.

* * *

As Trent headed for school on Tuesday, Kieran came out of a side street. They walked on together.

'Your mother asks sensible questions,' the skinny boy mumbled. 'Dad says so.'

Trent was only half listening. He was remembering the book-elf's words about going too far, doing more than the wish deserved. He wouldn't make that mistake this time.

* * *

'Rehearsals after interval,' Mr Masoe told Room 21. 'Performances after lunch.'

Interval came. No sign of the guitar Deena was supposed to get. Phew, maybe he could just be an air guitarist after all. Then he heard a shout. 'Trent! Got it!' The girl was heading towards him, waving something above her head while kids ducked. Trent gulped.

The rehearsal began. Trent stood to one side. He hadn't even picked the guitar up yet. He didn't know *how* to pick it up. Come on, Gene!

The first part went by. There were jokes and

I WISH

surprises. Then he saw Deena pointing at him. 'We welcome Strolling Sam, our guitarist.'

Briar and Baillee and Richie and Conrad all cheered like they were meant to. Trent's heart banged. His lips were dry. *Gene, where are you?*

The other Cougars were watching. He had to do something. He stretched out a hand for the guitar.

Straightaway, the same tingling he'd felt on the climbing wall streamed into his body. Power poured through him. He strode towards the rest of the group.

Somehow his mind knew the tune. Somehow his hands knew what to do. His fingers flew. The notes came clear and fast. It was working!

The Cougars all stared at him. The other groups of kids turned to look.

The tune danced and leaped. *Awesome!* Trent thought. *I'll never doubt Gene again.*

Somehow he knew that there was a tricky part ahead. Trent remembered the climbing wall and he remembered the book-elf saying 'You tried to do too much, eh?' His fingers paused and brought the music to a perfect stop.

* * *

Whistling and cheering, from all of Room 21. Deena and Conrad flashed him huge grins. Across in the Wolverines, Kieran nodded. Mr Masoe was clapping.

As the last bits of the play passed, Trent felt amazing. He wasn't going to be just ordinary any longer. He was going to be *extra*ordinary.

* * *

Deena talked away flat out as Room 21 filed back into the hall for a pre-lunchtime assembly. 'Awesome!' she told Trent. 'Can't wait for our performance!'

Trent sat, half listening to the notices. Cross-Country soon ... School Magazine ... Good luck to Room 21 with their plays.

The last one made Trent twitch. The wish is working, he reminded himself. Stay cool.

He couldn't eat much lunch. As he was wandering around, Richie and Conrad called out, and he went to sit with them and Kieran. This school isn't too bad, he thought. It'll be even better when *everyone here* sees that I'm special.

ELEVEN

Room 21 returned to the assembly hall straight after lunch. 'Okay,' Mr Masoe called. 'First group.'

It was the Wolverines, with their mad scientist story. At the end, they unrolled a big, black-and-white-and-red drawing of a nuclear explosion, and they all fell down. 'Kieran made the explosion,' they said, when they got up again.

Then came the Fluffybums' zombie play. The Panthers acted the legend of a great canoe rowed across the ocean. Trent's stomach was churning again. His wish would still be working, wouldn't it? Come on, Gene!

'Okay,' Mr Masoe called. 'Cougars.'

* * *

Deena the DJ Kool announced the concert. Richie, Briar and Baillee (the audience) cheered. Conrad the useless organiser got all the performers' names wrong. The audience booed. Deena bossed the organiser and the audience around, just like in real life.

Trent placed one hand on the guitar. No tingling in his fingers. What if the spell had run out? What could he do?

Then he saw Deena was pointing to him and heard the words, 'Our rambling guitarist.' He picked up the guitar, and instantly, the tingling power flowed through him.

Gene had done it. How incredible. I'm gonna be brilliant, Trent thought. I can do anything!

He played – even better than the first time. His fingers flashed across the guitar.

He didn't want to end. The really tricky part lay just ahead. The part he hadn't played last time. The part he ... he was going to play now! He could do anything!

Then a switch seemed to turn off. The power disappeared from his body. He stood there with a guitar in his hands, and no idea what to do.

* * *

It was like the climbing wall all over again. His mouth hung open. His hands fumbled. The Cougars stared. Some of Room 21 began to whisper.

If he played, would the power return somehow? He pulled at the strings, and a twanging sound came. Some of Room 21 began to giggle.

Trent stood, guitar in his hands, face hot and stomach heavy. He was going to be shamed forever.

Then Deena spoke. 'I told you he'd twist his wrist!' she shouted at Conrad. 'I told you he'd ping his strings! It's all your fault, you useless organiser!' Next moment, Deena and Conrad were acting out a furious argument, while the other three Cougars pretended to boo and whistle.

Trent tried to look as if it was all meant to happen. Somehow he joined the rest of the group when Deena and Conrad announced the concert had been cancelled, and that was the end of the play.

The Wildcats performed their skateboard play but Trent hardly noticed them. His mind kept tumbling and whirling. Why? Why?

Then Mr Masoe gave out the marks. Wolverines first – 'Great nuclear explosion.' Fluffybums second – 'You lot are natural zombies.' Cougars third – '*Very* interesting ending. You certainly had us fooled, Trent.'

Deena appeared in front of Trent. 'Give me the guitar. I'll take it back to the Music Room.'

Trent passed it over. 'I ... thanks. For ... for helping me with that mess-up.' She just looked at him and moved away.

* * *

He walked home with Kieran. 'Awesome guitar-playing,' the other boy said.

Trent shrugged. 'While it lasted.'

He made himself speak again. 'Liked your nuclear explosion picture.'

'Dad showed me how to do the black and red

together,' Kieran said. 'I've learned heaps from watching him.'

He turned into his street with a 'See ya'. Trent walked on. He'd messed things up even worse than his first wish.

* * *

The flat was empty yet again, so Trent went straight to the carton and pulled out *Works Naturally*. The figure inside was pretending to be asleep, but this time Trent ignored the fake yawn. He also ignored the teeshirt of a warty-faced figure with a bandaged toe and the words GOBLIN HOBBLIN.

'Okay,' he demanded. 'Try and talk your way out of this one.'

TWELVE

Gene gave a fake, green-teeth grin. He seemed less stuck to the page than before. 'The spell worked, didn't it?'

'For a while,' grunted Trent. 'Then it *didn't* work. Just like last time.'

'So what did you do wrong?'

Trent glared. 'Nothing!' The book-elf just watched. He seemed more serious than usual.

'Okay,' Trent muttered. 'I did try to play a part that I knew was tricky.' As Gene began to open his green mouth, Trent hurried on. 'But you kept saying I'd be all right! And it all went wrong. It's not fair!'

'Look,' went Gene. 'There are heaps of rules about

wishes and how long they last. You got carried away, Okay? So did I.'

He flapped a green hand at Trent. 'I want to get out of here, remember? I ... I might have promised too much.'

'Am I allowed any more wishes?' Trent asked finally.

The green mohawk nodded. 'Yeah. But don't keep rushing into things, eh? Think it out first.'

'Yeah,' went Trent after a while. 'Yeah, okay."

* * *

He spent the rest of Tuesday making his mind up about something. He finished *Out of Time*, where the boy ran in a big cross-country race, and seemed to dive across the finishing line into his own world again. Weird. But interesting.

* * *

'Brad's got some more paintings I want to see,' went Mrs Karam on Wednesday morning.

Brad? wondered Trent. Oh, yeah – Kieran's father.

He'd almost reached his classroom when he saw the person he was after. 'Hey, Deena?'

She stopped. 'What?'

'I'm ... I'm sorry about the play. Things went wrong. It's ... it's hard to explain.'

'Okay.' Deena looked at him. 'That was so weird. We just can't work you out.'

Yeah, Trent thought. Things could be easier if I was just my ordinary, boring self. But not yet. I've got an idea for another wish.

* * *

'Okay, you lot,' Mr M. told Room 21. 'I'm going to read you a new book tomorrow.' Pleased noises from the class. 'But first, *you're* going to sell *me* a book.' Puzzled noises from the class.

Their teacher grinned. 'You have 10 minutes to write me an advertisement for a book you've read. Tell us what it's about. Make it sound exciting. Go!'

I'm going to write about *Out of Time,* Trent decided. His ballpoint raced across the paper: the lonely guy; the weird accident; the different world; the big race. Words poured out.

'Stop!' called their teacher. 'Swap with someone else. Read as many adverts as you can. Give each one a mark out of 10.'

Richie had written about a tae kwan do book. Conrad's was a story where a dead man spoke to his son. Some girl had chosen a book about 'Being-A-Fashion-Model.' (No Way.) Another girl had picked one about collecting Barbie dolls. (*Totally* No Way.)

'Finish now,' Mr M. told them. 'Add up the marks. No, Deena, you can't have a calculator.'

'Okay, who's got an average of 10/10?' asked their teacher. 'Nobody? 9/10, then?' Baillee's small hand pointed to Trent. 'Him.'

'Good stuff,' Mr Masoe nodded. 'Another mark for the Cougars.'

The teacher read out Trent's advert: *Different universe ... mysterious girl ... cross-country team ... black clouds ... amazing ending.* 'You really got caught up in it,' he said.

I WISH

Trent's mouth started to move. He squeezed his lips shut. But five words escaped.

'I used to do running.'

THIRTEEN

It could have been worse, he thought as he trudged uphill that afternoon. But some of the class had looked at him again. Gene had to make *one* of his wishes work completely.

Kieran walked with him, naming the stars painted on his bag. 'Your mum knows plenty about them,' he told Trent. 'Dad reckons so.'

His mother had been mentioning Kieran's dad a lot, Trent thought. Mrs Karam wasn't home (again). So Trent went to the carton, lifted out *Works Naturally,* and began to open it. Then he paused, and went 'Knock, knock,' for some reason. When a voice squeaked, 'Wadda ya want now?' he opened

I WISH

the book and started talking to Gene about his third wish.

'So,' the green figure grumped. 'You wanna be an amazing runner. Simple as that, huh?'

Trent ignored the grumping. He also ignored the teeshirt with the warty-faced small creature riding a bike all over the place, and the words GOBLIN WOBBLIN.

'The school cross-country is next week,' he said. 'If I do really special in it, like the guy in the book, then ... then I won't want any more wishes.'

'What's so special about being special?' the book-elf asked. Trent shrugged.

'I'll need to check,' Gene said.

Aw no, thought Trent. 'You mean FLOB?'

'SLOB!' Gene squeaked. He looked hard at Trent. 'And you're gonna have to do some of this yourself.'

'How?' asked Trent. The green lips smirked and told him.

When Mrs Karam arrived home, Trent was

coming out the door wearing teeshirt and shorts. She blinked in surprise. 'Where are you going?'

'It's the school cross-country next week,' Trent muttered. 'I have to – I'm doing some training.'

He jogged downhill towards school – easily. But jogging back uphill *wasn't* easy. His chest heaved; his heart thudded; his legs wobbled.

Oh man, his third wish had better work. No way could he manage this running by himself.

How long till Gene heard from SLOB? Would they say, yes? Please let them. Just this last wish; that was all he wanted.

He started another book from the carton. It was called *Write On*, about a kid who was keen on reading, and helped with the school magazine. Slow, decided Trent. Not enough happening.

Mrs Karam left early on Thursday morning. 'I'm dropping in to see Brad's latest supernova painting. Have a good day, love.'

Trent headed for the carton. But as his hand touched *Works Naturally*, a voice snapped, 'Not yet!'

'I'm waiting to hear back,' the voice went on. 'You think I'm on call 24/7?'

'How long?' asked Trent.

The voice from the book replied, 'Two days. And make sure you keep doing your bit, eh?'

'Aw, no!' groaned Trent.

The voice sniggered. 'Aw, yeah! More running!'

* * *

He and Kieran plodded uphill together that afternoon. Trent's legs didn't feel too bad after yesterday. Walking to school each day was probably helping him get fitter, too.

'You said you'd done some running,' the skinny boy said. 'Where?'

'My school before this one,' Trent mumbled. 'Didn't mean to sound off about it.'

Kieran nodded. 'Just wondered if I'd seen you at some event. I run a bit, too.'

* * *

So that evening, and on Friday, Trent went running again. He ran in a different direction, away from school. It was hard, but he made himself keep going. Only a week till the school cross-country.

When he went to bed on Friday he read more of *Write On* – it was getting faster, and the stuff the guy wrote for the school magazine was quite funny. By then, two other things had happened.

First, his mother had said, 'Kieran's father says you're being a real friend to him. Good, love.'

Second, his wish about the cross-country had been granted. Granted, if ...

FOURTEEN

'I'll get a takeaway,' Mrs Karam had announced when Trent got back from his run, on Friday. 'Big Burger?'

As soon as the car spluttered off, Trent grabbed *Works Naturally.*

He could hear Gene inside, gasping, 'Up – two, three! Up – two, three!' The book-elf was doing sit-ups on the page. He certainly was less stuck to it than before. Gene glared. 'Thought I told ya to knock!'

'What are you doing?' Trent asked. The green figure showed pinhead-sized green muscles. 'Gettin' fit. I've got heaps to do when I'm out of here.'

The words echoed in Trent's head. *When I'm out of here.* 'You mean I'm allowed my wish?'

'No problem. SLOB know guts and talent when they see it.'

Trent grinned. 'Yeah, I've been training a lot.'

'I meant *me!* You're just a use ... ' Gene stopped quickly. 'A ... An interesting young human.'

'So, my wish is okay?' Trent asked. 'I *am* going to be a brilliant runner, like the guy in the story?'

The book-elf nodded. 'The wish is good for just one race, okay? There's a time limit on it. And you gotta keep training. You gotta keep doing your bit.'

'I will! Thanks, Gene!' Trent lifted one hand for a high five. The book-elf stared. 'You washed your hands today?' but he smacked Trent's palm with his tiny green one.

'You'll be let out after this spell?' Trent asked.

The book-elf nodded, and his mohawk shook. 'Better be. Now push off. I need to do more exercises.'

When his mother came home, Trent was doing

up his sneakers. 'I thought you'd already been for a run,' she said.

'Put my burger in the microwave,' Trent told her. 'I'm off for more training!'

* * *

Saturday, and still another run. Then Sunday morning Trent finished *Write On*. He was reading so many books! He liked the ending of this one, where the boy sent one of his stories to a magazine, and you were left wondering if it would be published.

His mother was in the living room, writing another science article when he finally emerged from his room. 'Do you know that artist guy's phone number?' he asked her. 'Brad?'

Mrs Karam's face seemed to go pink. 'Brad? Why?'

'I want to see if Kieran feels like going for a run.'

* * *

'Not too fast, eh?' Trent told Kieran when they met. 'I want to be fit for the cross-country, not dead.'

The other boy grinned. 'Okay.'

They jogged along streets, down and up slopes. Kieran talked quite a bit – for him. 'I think about paintings and stuff when I'm running. Do you think about books?'

When Trent stared, the skinny boy went, 'Well, you know heaps about them. In those class tests and things.'

I do? Trent thought.

The next hill was tough. His legs ached; his heart thumped. When they reached the top, he was glad to see the other boy was gasping, too.

'You wanna – come in?' Kieran jerked his head at the small house beside them. 'This is our place.'

A man was coming out of a garage at the end of the drive. 'My father,' Kieran told Trent.

Brad the Dad had paint on his teeshirt and arms. 'Want to see the supernova?' he asked Kieran, after he said Hi to Trent. 'It's nearly finished.'

Inside the garage, a big square of canvas stood on an easel. Trent stared at the giant star, its fire streaming out against deep, black space. 'Awesome!'

I WISH

Kieran's father showed him other paintings of moons, comets, galaxies. 'You ask questions just like your mum,' he grinned.

That was cool, Trent thought as he jogged home. And things will be even cooler when my third wish comes true.

FIFTEEN

'Where's Kieran's mother?' he asked at dinner.

Mrs Karam looked sad. 'She died when Kieran was little, love.'

Later, Trent took another book from the carton. It was called *World in Flames*. A bunch of kids working in a pine forest to earn money for a school trip are caught in a huge fire. Cool. Well – hot, actually.

* * *

Monday ... Tuesday ... Wednesday skimmed past.

School was okay. He, Kieran, Conrad and Richie ate lunch together every day now. 'Do you really do running?' asked Richie on Tuesday.

'Only if I'm late for school,' Trent said, before his mouth could go crazy. The others laughed.

'He's doing okay with training,' Kieran said.

Trent felt surprised and pleased. Richie nodded. 'If he's keeping up with you, he must be.'

I'm not just gonna keep up with Kieran, Trent thought. I'm gonna beat him ... aren't I?

* * *

On Tuesday and Wednesday, they had Personal Writing. 'Think of a down time in your life,' Mr M. suggested. 'An embarrassing time, maybe. When things felt bad.'

I'll write about when we came here, Trent decided. How I hated moving and having to start a new school. Before he knew it, words were pouring onto the paper.

'You could try sending some of your writing to the school magazine,' Mr Masoe told the class. 'Oh, and the magazine needs people to help organise stuff. Anyone interested? Deena – good. Hinemoana – good. Anyone else?'

The teacher's eyes moved to Trent, then moved on. Trent thought of the boy in *Write On*, who joined the school writing club, and sent his story off to a publisher.

He went running each afternoon, with Kieran or by himself. He was getting fitter and faster. Pity he hadn't started training earlier. But it didn't matter. His third wish would fix everything.

* * *

He finished *World in Flames*, with the trapped kids, and the forest fire roaring towards them. Be amazing to write something like that, he thought. Or have a book-elf to help you write it. He had to see Gene soon; make sure things were okay for Friday.

On Wednesday morning, his mother said, 'I'm out this afternoon, love. Back by tea.'

So Trent came home quickly after school. 'Knock, knock,' he said, as he picked up *Works Naturally*. He could still hardly believe what was inside.

'Wadda ya want?' The small figure was sitting up on the page, doing arm exercises.

'Just checking you're okay,' went Trent. The book-elf sniffed. 'Checking your wish is okay, you mean. Just remember you're on a time limit.'

Trent nodded. 'I will.'

'I'm thinking about *my* time, too,' went Gene. 'The time till I get outa here. I've told SLOB this is your last wish, so don't mess it up.'

Then to Trent's surprise, the book-elf said, 'You can talk to me again before the race – if you want to.'

SIXTEEN

Room 21 jogged the cross-country course on Thursday.

'No pushing – especially your teacher,' said Mr Masoe. 'No tripping – *very* especially your teacher.'

They trotted across the top field, down a walkway, along a path by the cemetery. The class talked as they jogged. Trent padded along beside Kieran. He felt good. Imagine how good he'd feel tomorrow.

They reached a slope where a steep bank dropped to the river. 'Careful here,' went Mr M. 'It's a long way down.'

Tomorrow I'll run to win, Trent thought. To be special.

'Good luck,' said Kieran as they reached his street after school. 'For tomorrow.'

'You too,' Trent mumbled. He headed home, feeling guilty.

* * *

'We're out of milk!' Mrs Karam called before tea. 'Want to come to the supermarket, love?'

'I'm ... I'm finishing a book,' Trent said. His mother smiled. 'You're becoming a great reader. Brilliant!'

Thirty seconds later, Trent opened *Works Naturally*. Today, Gene's green teeshirt showed a dragon breathing fire onto a bag of money, and the words DRAGONS ARE BAD FOR YOUR WEALTH.

'I had another run today,' Trent said.

Gene sniffed. 'You might need it.'

Trent stared. 'Why?'

'Wishes start losing power if you keep using them one after another, the way you have.'

The mean, green elf-machine was in a bad mood. 'What's wrong?' Trent asked.

'*You!*' snapped Gene.

Then the book-elf sighed. 'Sorry.' Trent blinked; Gene had never said that word before.

'I've got a lot hangin' on this,' the green lips muttered. 'Look, you'll be sweet. Just remember that wish won't last forever.'

This is my last wish, Trent thought as he lay in bed. My last chance to be special, to make people really notice me. It's going to work ... please –

* * *

Friday morning was cool with no wind. Perfect weather for running. And for worrying.

'Good luck, love,' his mum smiled. 'You've trained hard. You deserve to do well.'

Trent felt glad. He felt nervous, too.

He walked to school by himself. His legs felt clumsy; his stomach kept churning. That surge of power he'd felt with the first two wishes seemed a long way away. But it was going to come ... *double* please?

Personal Writing was before lunch. 'Today, you can write about an *up* time,' Mr Masoe said. 'A real or imaginary one, where things suddenly turn out good. Go!'

Trent started writing. A prisoner was trapped inside a building, trying to get away from a monster. Only at the end, when the prisoner escaped, did the story say that he was a trapped bird and the monster was a family cat. *Where did all that come from?* wondered Trent.

And then it was lunchtime.

* * *

He ate hardly anything. Neither did the other boys. Everyone was nervous.

The girls lined up. A starting pistol banged; and they streamed off across the field.

'Five minutes, guys,' a teacher called. Trent's brain sent urgent messages. Are you there, Gene? Are you watching? *Triple* please?

The girls had vanished into the distance, even the ones already walking. A teacher called the boys together. 'Okay, guys, line up.'

Trent was next to Kieran. His body kept twitching. Come on, Gene!

'Ready?' *BANG!* They were off. And instantly, the power came pouring into Trent. He felt as if he was running on springs. Yes! This was going to be it!

Across the field and down the walkway they went. Trent powered forward as they reached a level stretch.

They loped past the lines of trees flanking the walkway. Trent was keeping up with the leaders, no trouble. The energy seemed to be flowing even more strongly through his body.

Kieran was running smoothly, and Trent felt pleased to have his friend beside him. Yeah, that's right, he thought. My friend.

The steps to the cemetery were ahead. Trent began bounding up them. Oh, wow – the strength inside him!

Some girls were ahead, walking and talking. A couple from his class turned to look. 'Go, Kieran!' one yelled. Then – 'Trent! Go, Trent!'

The tricky downhill slope was ahead. After that, a clear run to the school and the finish. He'd hang back till the last 100 metres, then he'd go, take Kieran with him if the other boy could hold on. He was running on air. Thanks, Gene!

They reached the slope. Girls were picking their way down carefully. The leading group of boys slowed down too, moving to the safe side of the path. Kieran was just in front of Trent.

Then he heard the voice. 'Help!' His head jerked, towards the river. Nobody. Then it came again. 'Help! Please!'

He swerved across the path, peered over the edge. Deena and another girl lay there at the bottom of the steep bank.

SEVENTEEN

Kieran and the other boys hadn't heard They ran on. Trent stood, gaping down at the two figures. Deena was moving; the other girl lay still. Deena saw him. 'Trent! She's hurt. Help!'

His mind spun. He had to win; he had to think how much time was left.

'She slipped,' Deena was yelling. 'I grabbed her, but she pulled me over. She's broken her arm or something. Can you get us up?'

He couldn't. He had to run. The power kept pouring through him. The leading boys were 50 metres ahead now. They hadn't looked round.

'Get a teacher!' he told the kids who had joined

him at the edge. Next second, he was skidding down the steep bank.

The other girl was small and red-haired. She groaned. Her right arm flopped across her body.

Trent began helping her sit up. She groaned again.

'Quick!' he told Deena. 'Give me a hand.' Together they lifted the girl till she was half standing on wobbly legs. 'We're going to get you up the bank,' Trent grunted.

Deena held her by one elbow. Trent put an arm around her. Then they were all scrambling up the slope. Trent's legs pushed. The strength throbbed through him. But for how much longer?

Kids above gasped, 'Look at him go! That's amazing!'

Hands reached towards him. The girl was hauled up onto the path. She cried out as someone took her wrist. Deena and he struggled up after her.

'That was – incredible!' Deena panted. 'How – '
But Trent was already running.

* * *

He raced onto the last stretch of walkway, flying past jogging guys and walking girls. The power still rushed through his body. How much time?

The walkway turned right, between rows of trees. Another bend after that, he remembered, then the school entrance and the final stretch across the sports field.

Round the first bend he raced. He could almost hear the seconds ticking away. His own fitness was really helping.

He sped around the second bend. The school grounds were 200 metres ahead. Halfway towards them, he saw the leading runners.

* * *

Trent charged past another couple of boys. He was sprinting flat out, catching the leaders with every stride. How much time left?

Only Kieran and two others were ahead of him now. I can do it, Trent knew. I can do it. Kieran looked back. He saw Trent, and grinned.

Trent was just 15 metres behind, catching them with every step. He was going to win. He –

The power vanished from his body.

* * *

He staggered and almost fell. His legs were rubber; his arms heavy. Oh, no! Not again! It wasn't fair!

He forced himself on, trying to use the last of his own fitness. Kieran looked back once more. Trent waved the other boy forward. His friend raced away, over the finish line.

Trent stumbled on. His whole body ached. Feet thumped behind him. He tried to sprint.

It was hopeless. A figure tore past. Another followed.

The finish line was 10 metres away. Trent's lungs were agony. More feet raced up behind.

He staggered across the line, just ahead of the boy chasing him, and collapsed on the ground.

He wasn't first. He was sixth. Or maybe seventh. His last wish had turned into another disaster.

EIGHTEEN

He lay on the grass, panting. He felt empty and useless. He'd wasted his final wish. Now he'd never be special.

'Hey, Trent?' Kieran was standing there. 'You okay?'

Trent managed a nod. 'Yeah.'

'Did you win?' he asked as he struggled to his feet. Kieran nodded, too; he looked almost embarrassed. Trent felt a flicker of pleasure for his friend.

'What happened?' Kieran went. 'You were going brilliant.'

Trent shrugged. 'I messed up – again.'

He got changed. He could hardly drag his teeshirt over his head. Other kids kept looking at him – the guy who was a total failure.

* * *

When he creaked out of the gym, he saw Deena, talking to Mr Masoe. Trent sneaked away.

Halfway towards the front gate, he met Kieran. 'See you tomorrow?' the other boy said. Trent raised his head. 'You not coming home?'

Kieran looked embarrassed again. 'The newspaper wants to talk to the winners. They're doing a special article.'

Yeah, thought Trent, as he plodded on. Special. Not like me.

* * *

He could hardly make it up the hill. His legs ached. He felt empty and ordinary and useless, all at the same time.

His mother wasn't home again. How come she was spending so much time out of the flat just now? He could speak to Gene, but that would be useless, too.

Some little kid outside was whining about something.

No – the voice wasn't outside. It was coming from a book. A book called *Works Naturally*.

'Ya listenin'?' it squeaked. 'Come here, ya thick ... ya human! I wanna talk to you!' The book-elf was sitting almost upright on the page. Today's tee-shirt showed a dragon breathing on a troll. Flames poured from the troll's pants. PLEASE PUT OUT YOUR BUTTS, it said underneath.

Gene folded green arms and tapped a green foot. 'Well?'

Trent shrugged. 'I messed up.'

A green finger pointed at him. Its green nail needed cutting. 'I told you to watch the time! If a stupid human girl falls down a bank, does a stupid human guy need to help her?'

Trent shrugged again. 'Yeah, I know. Wasn't your fault.' He paused. 'You'll be able to get out now, though? PLOP, or whoever, will let you, won't they?'

To his surprise, the book-elf didn't get wild.

Instead, he said, 'Look, I've been talking to SLOB again. They know about the dumb ... the unusual thing you did during the cross-country. And some of them reckon you deserve another half chance.'

Trent gaped. The book-elf sighed. 'Man, you are *slow!* You might get another half wish.'

* * *

Not a wish that would do everything for him. A half wish that would do half the things for him. A bit less than half, maybe. According to Gene, some of SLOB weren't keen on granting anything.

He went to bed early, still aching all over. He picked up the last book from the carton and started reading.

It was called *So Long, Sam*, about a girl whose parents had split up. It helped – a bit – take his mind off how he'd messed up the cross-country.

And it helped stop him thinking about his half-wish. Funny: he'd been so excited about his first wishes. But he didn't feel very interested in this one at all.

* * *

Saturday morning. By 8 o'clock, Trent was up. By 10 o'clock, his mother had gone out. By just after 10, his weekend had changed completely.

'I'm going over to see Brad – Kieran's father,' his mum said at breakfast. 'There's something we ... we're sorting out. You'll be okay for an hour? Here's five dollars to get a pie at the dairy.'

Trent turned on his computer. Then he turned off his computer. He took the money his mother had given him and wandered off towards the dairy. He felt stiff, but not too bad, considering what he'd been like yesterday. Being fit must have helped. Be cool to be *really* fit. Maybe he could half wish for ... No.

He reached the dairy as Deena came out. The girl went 'Hi'. As Trent mumbled something, she went on. 'Tamsin says thanks.'

Trent looked blank. Deena said, 'The girl you helped. That was amazing, how you got her up that bank.'

Trent shrugged. 'I messed up.'

'Hey,' went Deena. 'You know I'm on the magazine committee? Can you send us that advert you wrote for the book – the one Mr M. read out? We need stuff really quickly.'

Suddenly, Trent knew what his third-and-a-half wish was going to be about.

NINETEEN

'A writer?' repeated Gene. 'A climber, a guitar player, a runner, and now you wanna be a writer?'

'Just for one story,' Trent asked. 'Just help me write one really special, super-cool story.'

Green teeth chewed a green bottom lip. Gene's teeshirt today showed a white-bearded, stumpy figure being shoved into the sea, and the words, PUSH A DWARF OFF A WHARF. Finally the green head nodded. 'All right, then. I'll ask SLOB. But remember – the S in their name stands for *"Scary".*'

* * *

Trent thought about his last wish all through Saturday. He was going to write a story for the school magazine. A story so awesome that everyone who read it would hold their breath.

But first, he had to find something to write about. And he had only half a wish to help him.

So, what *could* he write about? Come on – think!

Then just as he was turning out his light that night, he knew. Yes! Brilliant! Yes, he'd write about that.

* * *

He was planning to start his awesome, really-last-wish, story on Sunday afternoon. When the phone rang, he let his mother answer. 'Hello? Oh, hello, Brad. I'll get him.' Mrs Karam put down the phone. 'Kieran's dad, love. He wants to talk to you.'

'Hi, mate,' went Brad. 'Kieran and I are heading to the Astronomical Observatory. We've got some drawings to do there. Want to come?' Trent heard himself saying 'Yeah'. He liked Kieran; liked his Dad, too.

He went along – in a car full of sketch pads and paint tubes. At the observatory, they stared through a telescope at the Sun, with a dark filter so the sunlight didn't boil their eyeballs. Trent gaped at the things Brad and his son had come to draw. Sunspots: great dark storms across the Sun, twice the size of Earth.

Trent wished he could draw – No, he'd made his last wish. Anyway, he was going to do something special, too. He'd found his topic.

* * *

He walked to school on Monday with Kieran. 'Thought I'd see if the magazine wants any of the observatory drawings,' said the other boy. Trent thought again of his story topic. He'd better get onto it soon.

'Important notice about our magazine,' the principal said at assembly. Trent's ears went up. 'The committee need your poems and artwork and stories no later than Wednesday.' Oh, man! Trent thought. He'd better get into his story straight away. 'The cross-country,' continued the principal. Trent's heart went down. But he clapped with the others when Kieran's name was read out and felt pleased again for his friend.

'Now, a special mention. Trent Karam.' Trent's mouth flopped open. 'Trent could have been one of the winners, but he stopped to help someone in difficulty. Very well done, Trent.' More clapping. Clapping for him, Trent realised. He was special ... almost.

'Four points for the Wolverines from Kieran,' Mr Masoe announced back in the classroom. 'And two points for the Cougars from Trent. Those Cougars are running hot.' Cheers from the rest of his group. Deena grinned at him. Conrad thumped his shoulder. Ouch. Richie thumped his other shoulder. Ow. Trent suddenly remembered to squeeze his lips shut, but no voice seemed interested in mouthing off today.

Hey, he thought again, I could almost manage without my wish. No, he decided. One last – *half* a last – wish, and then he'd be there. Then he'd be totally special.

They began half an hour's Personal Writing, and Trent began on his final wish ever.

TWENTY

This must be the part he had to do by himself. Because it was *hard.* He wrote a sentence, crossed it out. He wrote it a different way, crossed it out again.

By the end of the half hour, he'd done just three paragraphs. But he wasn't worried. When his wish came, his story would be really special.

* * *

'You helping that girl,' Kieran said, as they walked up the hill. 'That was like, really cool.'

'You winning,' Trent replied. 'That was like, really cooler.' They both laughed. 'You doing anything for the magazine?' asked Kieran. 'You're good at writing.'

Trent's mouth opened. He squeezed it shut. It opened again. 'Dunno. I might.'

* * *

At home, he picked *Works Naturally* out of the carton. 'Knock, knock,' he called. A squeak came back. 'Come on, then!'

I'm going to miss Gene, Trent realised. When this wish was over, Gene would probably be free to go. What would it be like without the little green grumbler?

He opened the book. The book-elf seemed to sit back down quickly on the page. Today's teeshirt showed two giants pulling a fiery creature behind them. DRAGON DRAGGIN, read the words.

'Have you heard back?' Trent asked. 'From SLOB?'

Gene looked at him. 'You'll be right. Just ... when do you wanna have this story finished?'

Trent swallowed. 'Two days.'

The green eyes bulged. 'Two days??'

Trent swallowed again. 'Can't you do it?'

Gene stared at him. It was a different, careful stare. 'Look, read my green lips. YOU'LL – BE – RIGHT.'

* * *

Trent couldn't sleep. He lay in bed and thought. About his last wish ... his story ... his last chance to be special ... his story.

He'd already written the opening. He knew what should come next, and after that, maybe he could try ... Or he could use ...

He looked at the clock. 11.12 pm. He swung out of bed, turned on his light, and started writing. A sentence. Crossed out. Two more sentences. One crossed out. A paragraph. Another ... no, cross that out, too. 12.15 am: Oh, man! Three more lines. Yeah, this idea was better.

Then Trent sat up straight. He breathed in. Gene had done it! The power was inside him, quieter and more gentle than before, a soft, spreading glow.

He could do this. He *would* do this. He leaned forward and wrote on.

* * *

'Trent! Trent, what are you doing?'

Aw, push off, Gene! Trent groaned, felt the paper in his hands.

'Trent! Wake up, love! What's going on?'

His mother's voice. Trent sat up, yawning and staring. Staring at the paper he held, covered in his writing.

There were pages of it. He was slumped across his desk, his light still on.

He sat up and remembered. The writing, crossing-out, rewriting. The quiet, dark night outside. Pages filling up. The steady, gentle glow inside, as he wrote on and on.

He'd used up his last-ever wish. He'd finished his story.

TWENTY-ONE

'I ... I woke up early and thought I'd finish this.' Trent began grabbing the pages. 'I went ... went back to sleep.'

His mother laughed. 'Must have been *very* early. Looks like you've written a whole book!'

'Nah, just a story. I'll tell you later.'

* * *

He yawned his way towards school. A voice called, and Kieran came jogging to catch him up. Wouldn't have been right if I'd won the cross-country, Trent suddenly knew. Wouldn't have been fair. 'Been trying to finish the sunspot drawings,' the other boy said.

'That one of them?' Trent pointed to some rolled-up paper sticking out of his friend's star-painted bag. Kieran looked shy. 'Yeah.' He pulled out the drawing.

A huge sunspot, rays of white light pouring from its black centre. 'Awesome!' went Trent. 'Hey, I'd like to write a story about that.'

Kieran grinned. 'I could do drawings for other stuff you write, if you want.'

They walked on. Gene must have done an amazing job talking to SLOB. Trent could still feel last night's glow inside him, quiet and warm.

* * *

'Would you like to hear the book Trent wrote his advert for?' Mr Masoe asked Room 21. 'The *Out of Time* one? Can you bring along your copy, Trent?' Trent felt ... he felt cool.

Personal Writing next. 'Your second-to-last chance to do something for the magazine,' their teacher reminded them.

'And it has to be in by Wednesday, remember?' Deena went.

Trent read through what he'd written in the night. He added and crossed out. Gene, you're amazing, he grinned as the warm strength glowed inside him again. They've got to set you free after this. But how would he feel when that happened?

* * *

He hurried home, yawning again, to thank the book-elf. But his mum was there, chopping vegetables at the bench. She's not usually here at this time, Trent thought

'Why so much stuff?' he asked, nodding at all the food.

'Oh, Brad's coming for a meal. I invited him and Kieran.'

It was an hour before the other two arrived. Trent checked his story once more. He felt flat suddenly. Maybe it wasn't any good after all?

The others came. 'Kieran tells me you guys were

thinking of working together on some stories?' Brad said as they ate. 'Cool.'

* * *

Trent slept in. His mum had to call him three times.

'I'll be a bit late this afternoon, love,' she said at breakfast. 'I have to see someone. I'll bring something home for tea.'

He had to jog most of the way to school. He really was quite fit. He and Kieran could keep training together. In next year's cross-country, who knows ... ?

At school a small, red-haired girl went, 'Trent? Thanks for the other day.' Trent saw the wrist with plaster around it. Jasmin. No, Tamsin.

'Your arm, okay?' he asked. 'Sorry – stupid question.' The girl smiled. 'Yeah, it's fine, thanks.' They looked at each other. 'See ya,' she went. Trent mumbled, 'Yeah. See ya.'

Then he saw another person. 'Hey, Deena? I've ... I've got something for the magazine.' He held out his story. 'It's probably useless, but ... '

'Cool!' Deena went. 'We've got a committee meeting at lunchtime. We'll read it then.' She stuffed the pages into her bag. Careful! Trent thought.

* * *

Science. Maths. Personal Writing. Nothing left to write. Yes, there was. Kieran's drawings. A story about a giant, black sunspot. No, a Black Hole. A Black Hole that an alien race threw all their garbage into. Again, the ideas began to come.

At lunchtime, he and Kieran and Conrad were heading back towards Room 21 when a voice yelled, 'Hey, Trent!'

It was Deena. 'We – the magazine committee – we read your story,' she went 'And – '

Oh, no. Trent knew. It's no good. I'd felt so brilliant about it, and Gene got me my half wish, and I tried everything I could. But I'm useless, and it's –

' – It's awesome!' Deena exclaimed. 'Totally awesome! We'll publish it in the magazine!'

* * *

Trent couldn't pay attention in class that afternoon. His mind was full of his story. His last wish had worked. He had to get home and thank Gene. He'd miss that bad-tempered green face. He'd miss those wonderful glows that had filled him while he wrote.

He ran uphill towards the flat. He was fit, all right. As he turned into the drive, he saw his mother's car. She'd said she was going to be out! Now he'd have to wait to thank Gene. 'Oh, hello, love,' went his mother. 'I'm just off now to ... to talk with Brad.' Her face was pink. 'You know how I've been seeing him? How ... How would you feel if you and I and Brad and Kieran maybe lived together?'

TWENTY-TWO

After his mother drove off, Trent stood there with a stupid grin on his face. It was like having *two* wishes come true.

Suppose he still had another wish left: what would he use it for? He knew; he'd ask Gene to find where the carton of books had come from.

It was time to thank the book-elf. Thank him and say goodbye. He picked up *Works Naturally* and opened the book. Then, just like that first time, he dropped it. He caught it mid-air, and stared. The green figure had got free from the page. He was bouncing around, doing skips and star jumps. Today's teeshirt showed a book-elf escaping from a toothless vampire. The words read SO LONG – SUCKER.

'So BLOB or FLOB let you go,' grinned Trent.

But Gene didn't fire up. The book-elf took a breath and said, 'Trent. I – I'm sorry.'

'Sorry? What for?'

'For not getting you that last wish. The writing one.'

Trent stared. 'But I ... you ... what d'you mean?'

The book-elf's voice was serious. 'I really tried. But too many guys in SLOB reckoned you'd already had three wishes. Sorry. Did it mess things up for you?'

Trent's brain spun. 'But I wrote the story. They're gonna publish it in the school magazine! And I felt the power, like those other times. It was a lot quieter, but it was brilliant.'

Gene grinned, and all his green teeth showed. 'That wasn't the wish, dude. *You* did it. You made your own wish.'

Yes, I did, Trent realised. I did it all by myself. And that makes it so much better.

Gene stood up on the page. From a green pocket, he pulled a green comb and ran it through his green mohawk. 'How do I look?'

'Cool,' Trent told him. The book-elf looked pleased. 'Yeah, thought so.'

He gazed at the boy. 'See ya, Trent.'

Sadness rose in Trent. 'I – see ya, Gene.' The small, green figure lifted a small, green hand. 'Gimme five. Go *high*!' As Trent moved to touch palms, Gene pulled his away, and Trent missed.

The book-elf stuck his hand out again. 'Go *low*!' Trent reached, Gene pulled away, and the boy missed once more. The book-elf pointed. 'Look! Behind you!'

Trent whirled around. Nothing there. He turned back, and the page was empty. From somewhere, a squeaky, fading voice called, 'So long, *Human Sucker*!'

Trent closed the book. He was smiling.

* * *

'Dad told me about him and your mum,' Kieran said,

as they came down the hill on Wednesday morning.

'What d'you reckon?' Trent asked.

Kieran shrugged. 'No worries. Your mum's cool.'

Trent grinned. 'So's your dad. Yeah – no worries.'

'Hi, Trent,' said a voice as they reached school. He saw a plastered wrist. 'Hi, Tamsin,' he said. The girl's friends giggled. Trent didn't mind.

* * *

'Any more work has to go to the magazine committee by this afternoon, remember,' Mr Masoe reminded Room 21.

'Tell them we accepted Trent's story, Mr M.!' called Deena. 'Tell them it's awesome! Tell them what it's about!'

Their teacher laughed. 'Actually, Trent, *you* tell them what it's about.'

Trent looked at the floor. 'It's about this guy who wants to be special. He keeps mouthing off about the things he can do, but he messes things up every time. Till near the end.'

'Good,' smiled Mr Masoe. 'Another point for the Cougars, I think.'

Trent felt brilliant. Except for finding out about the carton of books, he couldn't think of anything in the world that he wanted to wish for.

* * *

Two people were at the flat when Trent arrived home. His mother and Brad.

'Well, mate,' Brad went. 'Sounds like you might have to put up with me and my noisy son for a bit. Hope that's okay?' Trent nodded. 'Yeah. Cool.'

His mother smiled. 'I have to go to the dairy again.'

She drove off. Kieran's father seemed to be making his mind up about something. He looked at the carton beside the couch. 'Those books are still useful, eh?' Trent stared. Brad grinned at him.

'They seem to turn up when people need them. They arrived in our house somehow, after Kieran's mum died. They helped a lot.'

Trent tried to speak. 'How – '

But Brad was talking. 'Then later, when we were okay, they disappeared. Now they're here.' He shook his head. 'Those books seem to have a mind of their own.'

Again, Trent tried to speak. 'What – '

'So,' asked Kieran's father. 'Was there anything ... interesting in them?'

Trent swallowed. 'Where – '

Brad smiled. 'Be great to have a carton of books like that always. Yeah?'

Now Trent smiled, too. 'Yeah,' he said. 'Yeah, I wish.'

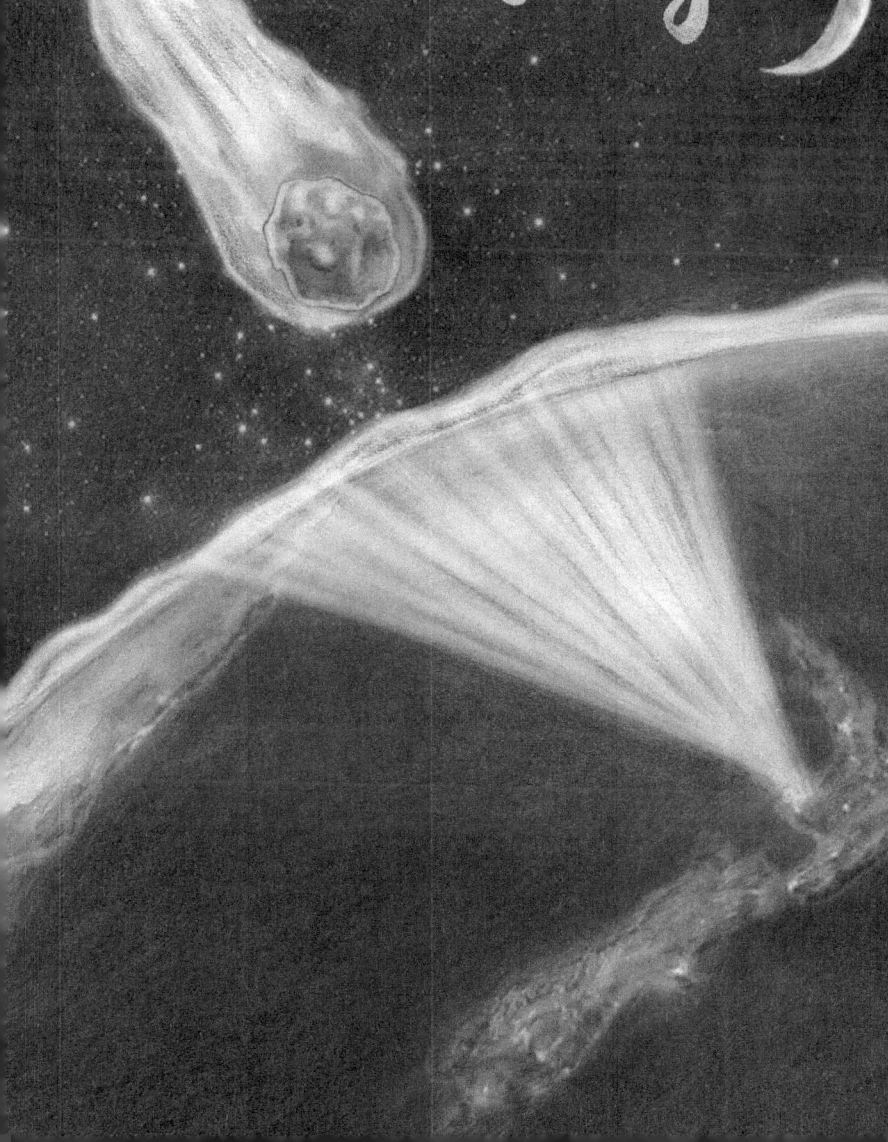

ONE

It's 70 million years ago. The great Milky Way Galaxy, with its billions of stars, slowly turns like a huge wheel in space.

One of those stars is yellow and bright, and eight planets curve around it. One of those planets is blue and green, covered with oceans and strange trees and mighty dinosaurs roam it.

Further out from the planets, huge rocks called asteroids drift around the yellow star.

Now another star slides through the Milky Way, past the yellow one. It is far away, but its gravity pulls at the drifting asteroids. Two of them change direction slightly. The star moves on.

The two asteroids slowly head towards the yellow star. The planets they pass also tug at them, and they change direction again.

A million years pass. Two million. Five million. On the blue and green planet, dinosaurs still roam and rule.

Every year, this planet makes one orbit around its yellow star. Then, one year, it comes sliding between the star and the two distant asteroids.

Now this planet's gravity also hauls at both giant rocks. One of them begins to move faster. And faster. It speeds, rushes, hurtles towards the blue and green planet.

On the world in front of it, a new day begins. Tyrannosaurus rex, Brontosaurus, Stegosaurus and other mighty beasts are feeding. Suddenly, a crackling sound grows above them. It swells into a roaring. A trail of fire flashes across the sky. The dinosaurs stare upwards, start to run.

Too late. A shape bigger than Mt Everest races

down towards the planet. It slams into the ground, smashing 40 kilometres through the planet's crust.

The whole asteroid explodes in a huge fireball. A shock wave tears outwards. Winds of 1000 kilometres per hour blast ahead of it.

The shock wave also hurtles upwards, sucking millions of white-hot rocks into the air. The roaring winds carry blazing fragments all around the planet. They start enormous fires wherever they crash to the ground.

Flames, earthquakes and tidal waves rage across the world. The fires burn for months, sending huge clouds of poisonous smoke into the air. The yellow star is blocked out. As the fires die, the planet grows freezing cold.

The mighty dinosaurs are wiped out. Only a few tiny creatures are left alive.

But in one place, something different happens. As the huge asteroid races down, a golden glow starts to spread across one small part of the planet below.

A deep humming grows. Flickers of light flow across the ground. Shapes seem to be inside them.

The giant tidal waves and earthquakes race around the world. As they reach the golden glow, they slow down, slide away. The blazing chunks of rock pour down from above, but they also skim away.

Days pass. Weeks, years. Slowly the planet heals. The tiny creatures that survived grow and change. Some begin to walk on two legs.

Nearly 70 million years later, the yellow star has a name. It is called the Sun. The blue and green planet is Earth. And the land protected by the golden glow is called Aotearoa New Zealand.

Meanwhile, out in the darkness of space, the second asteroid keeps drifting.

TWO

'Who's got a report to share?' asked Ms Li. 'Sophie? Come on, then, Rocket Girl.'

Room 4 laughed. Sophie didn't mind. After all, she was mad keen on anything to do with rockets and satellites and space missions. Plus her dad was one of the mission controllers at Mahoe Launch Site, only 5 kilometres away. And Mahoe Launch Site was where a mighty Neptune 3 rocket would blast off into orbit around the Sun in just 10 days. And she – Sophie Merrill – was going to see it happen.

She made her way to the front. Her friend Fatima stuck out her tongue, and grinned. Everybody looked interested. Everybody except for one person.

Pita Makereti looked angry. He always did when

anyone mentioned Neptune 3 and its Sunwind satellite. He's just jealous, Sophie knew.

So she didn't look at Pita. She looked at the rest of the class and began.

'Good Morning, everyone. My dad says the Sunwind Mission is on track for launch, just 10 days from now.'

Room 4 murmured. 'Ten days, Sophie?' Ms Li went. 'Amazing.'

Sophie felt proud. Her father had told her last night. All the rocket and satellite systems were working again, even though ...

'Things are all running properly,' she told the class.

'No, they aren't.' Pita Makereti was staring at her.

The class went silent. Sophie's mouth was open. How did – how could he know?

'What do you mean, Pita?' Ms Li asked.

The boy pointed at Sophie. 'Ask her.'

Sophie's face felt hot. Her father had mentioned it last night. Something had happened to

STRANGE MEETING

Sunwind. For two minutes, all its instruments went crazy. Lights flashed; alarms howled; computers shut down. Then everything started working again.

'Just for those two minutes, it was like some weird energy nearby,' Mr Merrill told his daughter. 'Then it stopped. Everything's been checked. Nothing wrong. Probably a safety switch kicking in when it didn't need to.'

He was silent for a moment. 'I've never known anything like it.'

* * *

The class was still watching her. Sophie swallowed. 'My dad says everything's been checked. There's nothing wrong.'

Pita was silent. His face didn't change.

'The first stage rockets will carry the Sunwind satellite into orbit around the Earth,' Sophie went on. 'Then its own engines will send it towards the Sun, at 20,000 kilometres an hour.'

Room 4 murmured again. Sophie felt pleased. She'd learned that figure off by heart.

'The satellite will send back data about the magnetic storms that pour out from the Sun. Just five minutes from one of those storms has more power than Earth uses in 100 years.'

'Fantastic, thanks, Sophie,' Ms Li said. 'Are there any questions?'

Fatima wanted to know what happened to the first-stage rockets. (They float down on parachutes, and get used again, Sophie told her.) Tyler Patu asked if a human could orbit the Sun some day. (They'd need a spacecraft with lead walls to protect them from radiation, said Sophie.)

Then Ms Li said 'Yes, Pita?' The boy's hand was up.

He looked at Sophie again. 'Tell us what the satellite's really going to be used for.'

THREE

'Sophie said,' Ms Li told him. 'It's going to measure the huge storms on – '

Pita shook his head. 'My koro, my granddad, he says lots of satellites are used for other things, too. Carrying weapons. Spying on people. Is your one?'

Sophie's face felt hot for a different reason. 'The missions my dad works on are good ones. Learning about space. Watching out for cyclones and forest fires.'

Room 4 were quiet for a second, then Ms Li went, 'Thank you, Sophie. Awesome. Who's next?'

Sophie sat down. She didn't look at Pita.

* * *

As she walked home that afternoon, she wondered. Why did the boy hate space missions? Who was the grandfather, the koro, he talked about? And how did Pita know there'd been trouble at Launch Control?

Before she turned into her street, Sophie stopped and stared out over the flat land near Mahoe Village.

There they were, in the distance. The low concrete buildings of Launch Control. The big grey signal dish, and, behind its high wire security fences, the Neptune 3 rocket.

It stood slim and white on its concrete pad, beside the launch tower. Even from this far away, Sophie could see the huge first-stage rockets; the snug shape of the Sunwind satellite on top. It's amazing, she thought. Beautiful. Can't Pita see that?

While Sophie watched, the light changed. A golden glow seemed to ripple over the rocket, the tower, the Launch Control buildings. It lasted a few seconds, then it was gone.

Sophie blinked. She stared at the sky. No clouds.

STRANGE MEETING

Nothing flying overhead. What was it? She kept watching. Nothing else happened. She turned and went inside.

* * *

'Dad, Mum, there's this boy in class who doesn't like space missions,' she said at dinner. 'Tell me again some of the really good things they do. Then I can tell him.'

Mrs Merrill was an electronics engineer. That's how she and Sophie's father had met. So while he cleared away the dishes, she told Sophie about the new cancer drugs developed in space, and the telescopes finding faraway planets where humans might live someday.

'And don't forget Sky Eyes,' she said. 'The satellites watching for any meteors or asteroids that might collide with Earth. They could save us from being wiped out like the dinosaurs!'

When Sophie went to bed that night, she felt pleased. She had answers ready for Pita Makereti. She'd tell him the truth. Him and his grandfather.

* * *

The middle of the night. Underneath Mahoe Village, the ground seems to murmur for a second, then goes quiet. Far above, satellites glide around the planet. Some watch the blackness of space, looking for anything that shouldn't be there.

Too far out for even the Sky Eyes satellites to see, the second asteroid still drifts. It's pulled one way by the Sun, another way by the big planets Jupiter and Saturn, a third way by Earth. It glides in this direction, then that. It could go anywhere.

* * *

Sophie was nearly at school next morning when she saw someone coming out of a side street. 'Pita!' she called. 'Wait up!'

The boy stopped and watched as she caught up with him. Two girls called 'Oooh, who's your boyfriend, Sophie?' Pita took no notice.

His brown eyes gazed at her. Sophie had meant to tell him the things her mum and dad mentioned the night before, but she heard herself saying something different.

'Why do you hate space missions? Why do you and your – your granddad have all these wrong ideas?'

Pita said nothing. Sophie's face started to feel hot again. He's so rude! He ...

Then Pita did speak. 'Why don't you find out what's really wrong? Come and meet him.'

FOUR

I will, Sophie decided as she sat at her desk. I'll go with Pita and meet his grandfather ... and his parents. I'll be polite, but I'll tell them the things Mum and Dad told me.

'Saw you talking to Pita,' Fatima whispered. 'He's cute, eh?'

Sophie blinked. 'He's weird!'

'Why – ' her friend started. But Ms Li was calling the register. Two rows away, Pita sat next to his friend Tyler. He hadn't looked at Sophie since he told her to come and see his grandfather. He'd just walked off and left her. He's weird and rude, Sophie decided.

STRANGE MEETING

Then she heard what Ms Li was saying. 'Sophie told us those amazing things about the Sunwind Mission. Well, I've been reading online that today, our Earth and Moon and the planet Mercury are all in a straight line. Their combined gravity will pull the Sun a hundredth of a centimetre towards them. So, watch out for the Sun skidding sideways today!'

Room 4 laughed. 'I saw that, too, Miss,' Megan Mills went. 'And they pull the big planets – Jupiter and Saturn – a whole centimetre closer, too.'

Then Pita spoke. 'My koro says Mercury is called Whiro. It means darkness, 'cos the first time people saw it, it was this little black dot crossing in front of the Sun.'

'The Moon is Marama,' went Tyler Patu. 'Its parents were Night and Sea.'

Pita smiled. Hey, Sophie suddenly thought, he does look quite cute after all.

'What's the Earth called?' asked Fatima.

'Papatūānuku.' Pita answered straightaway. 'The mother of all living things. My koro says we have to respect her. Not let rockets burn her body, and stuff like that.'

Quite cute, but still rude and weird, Sophie thought.

* * *

Little Mercury, just one quarter the size of Earth. The Moon, no bigger. Earth itself, so tiny compared to giants like Jupiter and Saturn.

But this day, three small shapes are lined up in a row. It lasts only a few hours, as they slide around the Sun.

Something else is lined up with them. The second asteroid feels the tiny pull of their gravity as it drifts past.

It changes direction. A few millimetres, then a few centimetres. A metre. Slowly it begins moving towards Mercury, the Moon, and Earth. Directly in line behind them for this short time shines the Sun, and its mighty gravity begins to drag at the asteroid, too. The huge rock moves a little faster.

Hours pass. The asteroid sails through black,

empty space, faster and faster. Far ahead, in a direct line, a little blue and green orb shines. The planet called Earth.

* * *

At lunchtime, Sophie told Fatima what Pita had said about meeting his grandfather.

'His parents are dead,' said her friend. 'Did you know?'

Sophie stared. 'How? When?

'Pita was only little. His father was a carver. He and Pita's mother were in the bush, looking for wood. There were special places they used to go. A tree fell on them.'

Sophie didn't know what to say. 'His grandfather brought him up,' Fatima went on. 'He's a carver, too.'

* * *

When Sophie crossed the road after school, a figure with hands in pockets stood waiting on the other side, watching her approach.

'You want to come now?' Pita asked. 'Meet my koro?'

Sophie swallowed. Things were happening so fast. 'I'll – I'll text my mum.'

They walked on. 'What you said about Mercury and the Earth,' Sophie went. 'That was cool.'

Pita nodded. 'My koro told me the names. He knows heaps about stars and stuff.' He stopped. 'Here.'

They were outside a small house with a grey roof. 'He'll probably be in his shed,' Pita said. 'Come on.'

Man, you're bossy, Sophie thought as she followed him around the side of the house. A neat, white shed stood behind it, and through the open door came a scraping sound.

'Koro?' the boy called. 'I'm home. And – '

'You've brought a girl from your school.' A quiet voice spoke. 'Come in.'

Sophie swallowed. How could he know that?

FIVE

The shed smelled of fresh wood, and pieces of timber stood, carefully polished and stacked, along one side. Sophie jerked as she saw a brown hawk staring at her, beak open, wings spread. Then she realised it was a carving. Beside it was a tuatara, with its spiny head lifted.

'Awesome!' she sighed.

The man standing by a bench smiled at her. He held a chisel. 'Thank you. I knew it was a girl. Boys clump along like they're in gumboots.'

Pita grinned. He was running his hands over the hawk. 'Nearly finished, koro?'

The man nodded. He had grey hair and a pair

of glasses were perched on the end of his nose. He smiled again. 'So you are Rocket Girl.'

Sophie's mouth gaped open. Pita's koro laughed. 'My grandson says you know so much. He asks me for things to change your mind. We need strong young people like you, with strong ideas.'

'I ... Pita knows a lot, too.' She hadn't meant to say it, but it was true. 'He told us these amazing names today.'

The grey-haired man looked at his grandson, and Sophie saw how proud he was. 'He is a good boy, even if his bedroom is like a rubbish tip.'

He looked at Sophie again. He seemed to be gazing right inside her. 'Your parents work on the Sunwind Mission.'

She took a breath. How did he find out these things?

Pita was still stroking the hawk's wooden wings and Sophie realised she could see every feather.

'I – ' she had to say something. 'Yes, Mr Makereti.'

The man laughed again. It made his whole face

change, like Pita's. 'You hear how polite our visitor is. Not like one grandson I know.'

He pushed his glasses up his nose. 'And your name is Sophie. Pita keeps saying it. "This girl Sophie. She's smart. I need things to tell her."'

His face became serious. 'Your parents are clever people, I am sure. Good people, too. They believe their space missions help the world.'

They were all silent for a second, then Mr Makereti spoke again. 'And some of them do. But there are other things that matter, too.'

His quiet voice became quieter. A little shiver seemed to run through the shed, as if the ground had shifted a tiny fraction.

'Our planet is so special, and this land is a special part of it. There is a power here. A power much older and stronger than us.'

Pita kept watching, one hand on the hawk.

'This power has helped us in the past. It will help again if we need it. But we must help it, too. We should not hurt this part of our Earth. Not burn it with rockets or tear up its skin for space bases. If we do, it may use its strength in other ways.'

He stopped and gazed at Sophie, then he smiled and waved his hand around the shed. 'Would you like to be a carver?'

All the things Sophie had planned to say about space missions were gone from her head. She gazed at the glossy hawk, the tuatara, then the other shapes nearby – a wide-eyed morepork and a tui curved in flight. 'They're amazing.'

'My son – Pita's father – he was a fine carver.' Mr Makereti sighed, then pointed to his grandson. 'So can this one be, if he keeps off his computer games. Pita, have you peeled the potatoes for tea?'

'I better go,' Sophie went. 'Thanks so much, Mr Makereti. See ya, Pita.'

'See ya, Sophie,' the boy replied.

That's the first time he's said my name, she thought. She quite liked it.

* * *

As she got near her place, Sophie stood and gazed

STRANGE MEETING

across the flat ground at the distant Mahoe Launch Centre. The Neptune 3 pointed at the sky and on the ground near it moved a few ants and beetles. People and vehicles.

The sunlight changed. It swelled into gold, just like the day before, then flickered like fire. It danced upwards, past the top of Neptune 3 and its launch tower, before vanishing into the high, blue sky. Must be reflections, Sophie decided this time. I'll ask Mum and Dad.

She walked on. That was cool, meeting Pita's grandfather. Maybe if Mr Makereti knew more about Sunwind, he'd feel differently. She wouldn't mind seeing him again. She wouldn't even mind seeing Pita again.

Off on the plain, the rocket gleamed. Just eight days to go.

* * *

The golden glow speeds out into space. It flashes on at the speed of light, till it reaches the enormous asteroid heading towards Earth.

The huge rock slows down. The gold surrounds it, then fades. The asteroid picks up speed again. The blue and green planet lies straight ahead.

SIX

Her mother was getting out of the car as Sophie arrived home. 'Hello, love. Your dad had to stay behind. Sudden message about something.'

Mrs Merrill unlocked the front door. 'Where have you been? Fatima's?'

'I went to Pita Makereti's place. He's in our class. His grandfather's a carver. He's awesome.'

Her mother watched her. 'Mr Makereti came to the meetings when Mahoe Launch Centre was being planned. Told us how special this place is, how sacred. Asked us not to harm it. Interesting man. His grandson – Pita. What's he like?'

Sophie wasn't sure what to say. 'He's okay. Got

some weird ideas about space missions. But ... yeah, he's okay.'

* * *

Sophie's dad texted while her mum was getting dinner. 'He's going to be late,' said Mrs Merrill. 'Said to start without us.'

Sophie was thinking about Pita's grandfather. Our planet is so special, he'd said. Yeah, Sophie knew he was right. But space is special, too. Pita's wrong when he says we should stop Sunwind and other missions. We have to keep learning about the amazing things out there.

It's really sad about his parents, though. What would I do if that ever happened to my mum and dad? Things have gone wrong on space missions. Rockets have blown up on the launch pad or taken off only to crash straight down again. That power Mr Makereti was talking about, how it might do things we don't expect ... No. No, I mustn't start thinking stuff like that.

* * *

STRANGE MEETING

Her father didn't come home till they'd nearly finished dinner. He looked tired. Tired and worried.

'What's going on?' Sophie's mum asked, when Mr Merrill finally sat down at the table.

Sophie's dad shook his head. 'Can't understand it. You know how our base radar checks the sky for anything that might cause problems at launch time – planes off course, flocks of birds, anything like that.'

Mrs Merrill nodded. Sophie listened.

'Well, these tiny shapes suddenly showed up on the screens. Heaps of them. Radar operators said they'd never seen anything like it. They were there for just a few seconds, then shot straight up at this incredible speed. That's why they kept us behind, to try and work out what it was. But nobody can.'

A prickling ran through Sophie's body. It must have been when I was coming home, she realised. When I saw that golden light, and the flickering. How ...

Her father was still speaking. 'So, do we stop the

Sunwind countdown till we find what it was? There was that other weird business, too: the instruments all failing.'

He looked at his wife and daughter. 'It's almost like something's trying to contact us. Trying to show us something.' He shook his head. 'It can't be that. No way.'

* * *

High above Earth, among the satellites floating around the planet, cameras and sensors scan the sky. They search for anything moving towards our world. Anything that may collide with it, bringing fire and death like the asteroid of 65 million years ago.

The second giant rock is still too distant for them to see. But every day, every hour, it gets closer. And faster.

SEVEN

That night, Sophie stared out her window towards the distant Mahoe Launch Centre. She couldn't see the rocket or buildings, but a pale glow lit the sky. Crews would be working there, running check after check on the mission.

It'll be okay, she told herself. Every mission has problems. They all get sorted.

But those things on the radar. They sounded so strange.

* * *

No sign of Pita on the way to school and he didn't look at her in class. 'What were you and Pita talking about yesterday afternoon?' Fatima asked at interval. 'Saw you on the footpath.'

'I met his granddad,' Sophie said. 'He does all these amazing carvings.'

'He gave one to my mum and dad.' Her friend's words made Sophie stare.

'Soon after they arrived here. This awesome eagle, like they have back home. Mum says he must have somehow known they felt homesick. It was like he could read their minds.'

Sophie remembered the things Mr Makereti seemed to know about her yesterday, and her back prickled again.

* * *

The asteroid moving towards Earth is bigger than the one that destroyed so much life on the planet all those years ago.

It has the power to shatter mountains, wipe out whole countries, send huge tsunamis racing right around the world. If it hits, it will turn the ground into boiling red-hot waves for thousands of kilometres.

It speeds on. Faster and faster.

* * *

Pita didn't take any notice of Sophie that afternoon, either. But after school, as she began crossing the road, the boy was there again, watching her come.

'My koro wants to know if your parents are all right.' Sophie stared. 'What do you mean? Of course they are.'

Then she remembered how tired her father looked last night. Tired, and worried about the strange things that were happening. And her mother was worried, too.

'What do you mean?' she asked again.

Pita shrugged. 'Don't ask me. I'm just saying what my koro told me to say.'

This guy was so unfriendly. Sophie opened her mouth to tell him, but Pita spoke first. 'I heard him talking in the shed after you left. Then this morning, he told me to ask.'

'Talking? Who to?'

Pita was gazing at the ground. 'He does it sometimes. And – and a few times there's this sound, like a voice speaking. A really deep, slow voice. But there's nobody there. Just him.'

The boy glanced at her, then down again. He's frightened, Sophie realised.

'My koro knows things,' Pita said. 'Before they happen, sometimes. He felt something was going to happen to Dad, that day – that day he and Mum were killed. He reckons he should have stopped them from going.'

'How does he – ' Sophie started.

Pita glared at her. 'I don't know! There's things nobody can understand. He told me so. Just because you like that stupid space stuff, you think you can find out everything.'

Now Sophie glared. 'It's not stupid!'

The boy shook his head. 'Look, after you left yesterday, this weird thing happened. It was like something came up from the ground, from deep down. There was this light that seemed to go everywhere. My koro stood still, like he was listening. Then he sent me inside, and I heard him in the shed, talking.'

He swallowed. 'But there was nobody else there. Nobody you could see, anyway.'

He looked at Sophie again. 'So he wanted me to ask you. Are your mother and father okay?'

When she spoke, Sophie's voice sounded strange. 'Something happened at the base.'

She described the shapes on the radar that her father had seen. 'Dad says nobody's ever known anything like them. He reckoned it was like something was trying to make contact. But that's impossible.'

Pita kept looking at her. 'Nothing's impossible. My koro understands that. You think you're so smart, you and your stupid space mission. You don't understand anything! You better watch out, or you'll find out the hard way.'

He turned, and stamped off.

* * *

Around the Earth, Sky Eyes satellites speed on their way. Cameras and sensors stay aimed towards the darkness of space. Nothing there to worry about. Nothing ... yet.

EIGHT

Sophie stamped away, too, all the way home. She'd never met anybody who could make her as angry as Pita did.

Then she thought of his parents. How scared he'd looked when he talked about that voice in the shed, and the light. She felt a bit less angry.

* * *

Her mother and father were home early. 'Everything back to normal,' Mr Merrill told her. 'Must have been an instrument blip on the radar. Countdown's going ahead.'

'Did you talk to Pita?' her mum asked.

'He's so rude!' Sophie went. 'And he keeps on about weird voices and lights he reckons are happening. His grandfather thinks they're something special.'

To her surprise, Mr Merrill nodded. 'Mr Makereti is pretty special, too. He knows a lot about astronomy. When we were talking about setting up Mahoe Base, he took us outside and showed us how the stars are like a great carved canoe in the sky, with anchor and rope and everything. Amazing.'

'He told Pita that space missions harm the planet,' Sophie said. 'That's not fair!'

'They could do harm.' Her mum spoke this time. 'Some countries want to put nuclear weapons in orbit. Some rockets carry nuclear fuel. I understand why Pita's granddad worries. Be good if we could all work together, treat space and Earth carefully.'

Yeah, thought Sophie in bed that night. But how do you work together with someone as rude as Pita Makereti?

* * *

The huge asteroid moves faster and faster. Straight ahead of it, the green and blue planet turns.

STRANGE MEETING

In space, there is no air to slow the huge rock down. If it enters Earth's atmosphere, it will glow red-hot, then white-hot. It will become a hurtling mountain of fire. A shock wave of air will charge ahead of it, destroying trees, buildings, all life for thousands of kilometres on every side.

* * *

Sophie's parents both had a day off work. 'Sunwind's countdown can manage without us for a bit,' her dad grinned. 'Just six days till launch. This satellite is going to travel so far, Sophie – 120 million kilometres towards the Sun.'

I *am* going to talk about this to Pita, and his koro, Sophie told herself as she left for school. I *will* get them to listen.

She came round the corner, and Mr Makereti was walking towards her.

* * *

The man smiled. 'Hello, Sophie. Pita told me you and he had another talk yesterday.'

Not really a talk, Sophie thought. More like a ... a war.

'It's good for him to listen to others.' Mr Makereti looks so sensible, Sophie thought. Not like a man who talks to weird voices.

She stared at Pita's grandfather's next words. 'Pita respects you, even if he does argue. Your mother and father should be proud of you. I'll tell them so.'

He nodded and walked on. So did Sophie. He's going to see Mum and Dad, she understood, but how did he know they'd be home?

* * *

'We've been talking a lot about space,' Ms Li told Room 4 next morning. 'Let's talk about Earth for a change. Our little piece of Earth. What's the best thing about Mahoe?'

'The space base,' said Rajan. 'The bush,' said Megan. 'School,' said Fatima, and everyone groaned. 'Me!' said Tyler, and everyone groaned louder.

Pita's hand was up. 'I like the way it feels special.'

People nodded and murmured. Why can't he be like that all the time? Sophie wondered. Why can't he stop being rude?

At interval, she and Fatima were outside, talking. Pita came round the corner. 'Saw your granddad this morning,' Sophie began. 'He was – '

The boy didn't speak. He didn't even look at her. He walked straight past. So Sophie didn't look at him for the rest of the day, either.

Then as soon as she reached home after school, she knew something had happened.

NINE

400 kilometres above Earth, a Sky Eyes satellite orbits the planet. Everything is normal. Everything is safe.

And then ... a light winks on one of the satellite's computers. It winks again. Cameras swing towards an area of sky. Inside the satellite, other computers begin to hum. Something has been seen. Something strange.

* * *

Mr Merrill was chopping vegetables when Sophie got home. Mrs Merrill was on her laptop. 'Hi, love,' ... 'Hey, Sophie,' they went, but their faces were serious.

'I met Pita's granddad this morning,' Sophie said. 'Did he – '

'He told us,' went her mother.

'So he came here?' Sophie asked. 'Why?'

Mr Merrill glanced at his wife, who nodded. 'He came to warn us.'

Sophie stared. Her mum spoke quietly. 'He says something might happen. "A great change," he called it.'

'What sort of change?' Sophie asked.

Mrs Merrill shook her head. 'He can't be sure. But he told us to be careful. He said there's a power of some sort in this place, and it's behaving strangely.'

Sophie's back prickled again. She remembered Pita in class that morning, talking about Mahoe being a special place. She remembered those flickers of golden light.

Her mother was still speaking. 'We're telling you because Mr Makereti feels you should know.'

Her father went, 'Sophie, there are people who have silly ideas about space. Pita's granddad isn't one of those. He knows ... he seemed to know about

Mission Control radar showing those shapes yesterday. And about the power failure before that.'

'Did you say anything to Pita, love?' her mother asked. 'We're not blaming you. We just wondered.'

'I – no, not really.' The voice, Sophie thought. The voice Pita had heard speaking to his koro. Should she mention that?

'As I said before, Mr Makereti's a special man,' her dad went. 'And he wants to help, even if he doesn't agree with Sunwind, and other things we're doing.'

'So we've spoken to Launch Control.' Sophie blinked at her mother's words. 'We've told them there might be an issue of some sort that could affect Sunwind.'

'They wanted to know what it was, of course,' Mr Merrill said. 'We felt a bit silly saying we didn't know. But then Mr Makereti asked to speak to them, and ... well, they took notice.'

Yeah, Sophie thought. Pita's granddad is like that. You take notice of him.

'So they're running extra security checks.

They're increasing patrols at base, till the launch is complete. Not bad for one man's warning, eh?' Her father smiled, but he still looked anxious.

'Don't worry, Sophie, love.' Mrs Merrill tried to smile. 'Your Dad's right – Mr Makereti is a special man. A good man. We want him on our side.'

Am I worried? Sophie wondered later. No. Yes. Not really. Sort of. Mum's right: I'm glad Pita's koro is on our side. I'm glad Mum and Dad are, too, if that makes any sense. Put them together, and they make an amazing team.

* * *

Messages have begun speeding among all the Sky Eyes satellites. The first one has passed around the other side of Earth now, skimming along in its orbit. But those satellites facing out into space, away from the Sun, are searching the darkness with every instrument they have.

A second satellite sees the same thing. A third and a fourth. There's no doubt. This isn't a false alarm. This is what the Sky Eyes were made for, why they were flung into orbit above the blue and green planet. It's what everyone hoped would never happen.

Now a message is beamed to Earth. The terrifying news flashes down to the world below.

TEN

Sophie walked to school next morning with her mind made up. She was going to speak to Pita; ask what Mr Makereti meant about 'a great change'.

She caught up to the boy as they were heading into morning assembly. 'Can I talk to you?' she asked. 'It's important.'

Pita gazed at her. He looks different, thought Sophie. Tired. Worried. 'Interval,' he said, then he moved on.

She waited for him outside Room 4 as interval began. She ignored the other kids grinning at them. Fatima stopped, then moved away. I better tell her what's happening, Sophie decided – if I can work it out myself.

'Your koro came to see my parents yesterday,' Sophie began, as the two of them wandered across the playground.

Pita nodded. 'He said.'

'He told them something's coming. A – '

'A great change. Yeah, that's what he said to me.'

As Sophie started to speak again, the boy held up his hand. 'I don't know what he means. I don't think he does, either, but something's happening, all right.'

He was silent for a second. 'He was in his shed for a long time last night. I heard him talking. And that light was there, too. Not always, just now and then. I didn't go to look. I ... I didn't think he'd want me to.'

The two of them watched each other. Pita's brown eyes were serious. He's not frightened now, Sophie realised. But something important is coming. He doesn't want to talk more about it. Not yet, anyway.

She waited, but the boy stayed silent. 'Will you

tell me if you find out?' she asked, and waited for Pita to snap at her.

He didn't. Instead, he nodded. 'Yeah.' Then he went, 'And you tell me if ... ' His voice trailed away. He turned and walked off.

Sophie stared after him. Tell him if ... what? She swallowed, and hugged herself. Mr Makereti wasn't frightened, but she was starting to be.

* * *

All across Earth, data is pouring into space headquarters. Lights flash. Alarms howl. Operators rush to their screens. They stare and gasp.

There it is, speeding towards them from deep space. It is still far away, but it's enormous. It's on a collision course with the blue and green planet.

The computers check and check again. There is no doubt. Impact will come, just over two days from now.

* * *

'Anything happening at the base?' Sophie asked at home.

Mrs Merrill shook her head. 'Everything's normal, love. We've listened to what Mr Makereti told us, as I said. Mission Control is doing the things we told you.'

Should I mention what Pita said? Sophie wondered. But her mum was still talking. 'A lot of hiccups can happen on a project like Sunwind, but we've got heaps of experts to sort them out.'

Sophie went to bed feeling more relaxed and in the morning, her parents seemed relaxed, too.

'Have a good day, love,' her father said as Sophie was leaving, 'I'll – ' his phone chimed. 'Whoops, better take this text. See you later.'

* * *

Everything seemed ordinary at school, too. Fatima teased her a bit about talking to Pita. Sophie wondered again if she should tell her friend what she and the boy had been talking about. No. No use upsetting people if there's nothing happening after all.

Maybe Mr Makereti was wrong. That light could

STRANGE MEETING

have been anything. Maybe he talks to himself in the shed? He's probably still upset about what happened to Pita's mother and father.

She and the boy met in the classroom doorway. 'Anything happening?' Sophie asked.

'Nah.' Pita didn't look at her. Oh, great, Sophie thought. He's back to being rude again. Things must be normal, all right.

* * *

Room 4 watched a science DVD on dinosaurs. The colossal monsters ruled Earth for 90 million years, the DVD said. Then an asteroid bigger than a mountain slammed into the planet. Fires and tsunamis and other disasters wiped out nearly all life.

Only tiny animals living in caves and burrows survived. As huge stretches of time went by, these animals became most of the creatures living on Earth today. 'We were lucky we had those burrows to protect us,' the DVD joked.

'All right, you pterodactyls and tyrannosauruses,' Ms Li went, when the programme finished. 'Now that you're experts, you're going to write me a page on ... '

Room 4 all groaned together. Their teacher laughed. 'You sound as if you're going extinct, too. You can – '

She stopped. A sound had started up in the distance. A shrill, wailing sound, growing louder, rising and falling.

The class stared at one another. 'What's that?' voices asked.

Sophie sat still. Her breath stopped; her skin crawled. She knew what it was. The emergency siren at Mahoe Launch Site. The siren that sounded only if there was sudden danger.

ELEVEN

Room 4 sat totally still. The siren wailed on, rose, then died away.

Ms Li was silent for a moment, then smiled. But it didn't look like a real smile.

'Probably a safety practice. They have those at the base, don't they, Sophie?' Sophie swallowed, and nodded.

'I'm feeling generous,' Ms Li went on. 'So we'll leave your writing project for a bit. Instead I'll read you the next chapter of the Time Traveller story you've been listening to, okay?'

As their teacher began reading, Sophie could feel the class starting to relax. The siren was quiet. Yeah, could just have been a practice.

There was a knock on the classroom door. Mahoe School Principal, Mr Pelisi, appeared. Sophie's stomach went tight as she saw how worried he looked. 'Ms Li, could I have a word?' he asked.

Their teacher stepped out into the corridor. There were noises from other classrooms. Sounds like kids leaving, Sophie thought. Can't be. It's half an hour till interval. She and Fatima gazed at each other, and Sophie realised her friend was scared.

Ms Li came back in. Her face was pale. Sophie's heart began to thump.

'Right, people,' their teacher said. 'Listen carefully, please. School is closing for the day.'

Noises from the class. Ms Li lifted a hand. 'We want you all to go home. If there's any problem with that, see me. The ... The Prime Minister has some important news. She's going to speak on TV and the radio at 11 o'clock. Off you go. Be careful.'

Room 4 filed out. Hardly anyone talked. Fatima held Sophie's hand for a moment, then left. There was no sign of Pita.

STRANGE MEETING

It's something to do with what his koro said, Sophie thought. The 'Great Change' he talked about to Mum and Dad. It's happening. And it's something bad.

* * *

Cars were arriving outside the school. Some arrived fast, skidding to a stop. Parents jumped out, searching for their kids. Voices called, nervous and anxious.

Sophie began hurrying along the footpath. She glanced at her watch. 10.45.

She was halfway home when a car pulled up beside her. 'Here, love!' her mother called. 'Get in!'

Sophie slid in. 'What's happening?' she demanded. 'Why was the siren going?'

Her mother stared straight ahead as she pulled away from the kerb. 'We'll talk when we get home.'

Suddenly a car turned, right in front of them, and she had to brake hard. They were passing the supermarket, and its parking lot was jammed with cars. People were rushing inside. Others were hurrying out, arms full of bags. She could hear distant voices raised and horns blaring.

'What – ' she began, but her mum was talking. 'Dad's at the base. He might be there a while. You're okay, love; I'll look after you.' The words made Sophie more frightened.

Inside the house, her mother held Sophie's shoulders, and sat her down on the couch. Her hands were trembling and Sophie realised she was shaking, too.

Her mum flicked a look at her watch. Sophie did the same. 10.52.

Mrs Merrill took a deep breath. 'The Sky Eyes network has picked up something headed towards Earth. We don't know what it is yet. It's still a long way away. It might be a false alarm. The gravity of anything it passes could make it change course.' We were talking about that in class, Sophie remembered, just two – no, three days ago.

Her mother looked at her watch again then turned on the TV.

STRANGE MEETING

There was no normal programme on the screen. Instead, a notice read BREAKING NEWS. THE PRIME MINISTER WILL SPEAK AT 11 AM.'

Mother and daughter sat, holding hands. Neither spoke. Sophie's heart kept thumping.

The screen changed. The Prime Minister's face appeared. She looked calm and her voice was quiet.

'Tēnā koutou. Good morning, everyone. I'd like you to listen carefully to what I say. It's important we all understand what's happening.'

Sophie swallowed again. The PM went on, still quietly.

'The Sky Eyes satellites, the ones that watch for unidentified objects in space, have picked up what appears to be an asteroid headed in our direction.'

The PM raised a hand, just as Ms Li had done. 'I say "in our direction" because we don't know yet if it's on a collision course. It may miss us by a long way. But it's important we take all the safety precautions we can.'

This is what Mr Makereti meant, Sophie realised.

Somehow he knew. The voice and that light. They ...

The PM's voice talked on while Sophie tried to listen. 'Stay calm ... listen to TV and radio ... check your cellphone ... all schools are to remain closed for now ...and only essential services may remain open. This may change at short notice. In the meantime, please go home ... '

Then the words that made Sophie's body go cold. 'If your house has a basement or a cellar, take some food and water to it now, enough for several days if you can.. If you have no basement, but your neighbour ... '

Mrs Merrill pressed the remote and the PM's face vanished. She put her arms around her daughter, and held her tight.

* * *

The asteroid hurtles on. The green and blue planet ahead grows steadily bigger.

The Prime Minister is wrong. This asteroid will not miss Earth. It's racing straight at it; less than two days away.

TWELVE

Mr Merrill arrived home three hours later. Sophie and her mum had turned the TV back on, but there was nothing new, only the Prime Minister's speech repeated a couple of times, in between the usual programmes.

Her dad hugged them both tightly.

'New data?' Mrs Merrill asked straightaway.

Her husband shook his head. 'They're checking its speed and direction all the time. There's ... there's no change.' Sophie saw the way her parents stared at each other, and her stomach went tight again.

'Isn't there anything we can do?' Her own voice

sounded strange. 'Can't someone send up a nuclear missile or something, blow the asteroid to pieces before it reaches us?'

Her father stroked Sophie's cheek. 'They may try that, love. But nuclear missiles can't reach that far into space, and it could mean hundreds of pieces hitting us, instead of one.'

They stood silent. 'There are all sorts of experts working on it, love,' her mother said. 'Heaps of clever people. They'll think of something.'

Sophie was silent. She knew from her Mum's voice that she didn't believe what she was saying. The asteroid was coming, and there was nothing anybody could do.

* * *

While the asteroid hurtles closer, something else is also moving. All those millions of years ago, when the first great rock slammed into earth, something came rippling upwards from inside one part of the planet. It spread into the sky, holding back some of that terrible explosion. That something is stirring again.

STRANGE MEETING

The colossal asteroid charges straight on. Its surface is black and frozen, scarred by collisions with others. If it enters Earth's atmosphere, that surface will plough into the planet like an enormous axe, tearing the surface apart for thousands of kilometres.

Just over one and a half days to go.

* * *

Sophie and her parents were sitting silently on the couch, arms around one another, when her father's phone chimed. He listened, went 'On my way', turned to the others.

'I have to get back to base. Someone's got ... an idea. They want me there.'

He hugged Sophie and her mother again. 'Stay here. Be safe. We'll talk about a place to shelter when I get back.' The car drove off.

It's getting nearer every second, Sophie knew. There's nothing anybody can do. It's going to wipe out everything and everyone I know. Fatima and all the other kids. Mum, dad. Me.

Her whole body shook. She stood, so suddenly that her mother stared. 'I'm going to Pita. Pita and Mr Makereti.'

* * *

For a moment, she thought her mother might grab her, hold her back, but instead Mrs Merrill's arms reached towards her daughter, then stopped. She gazed at Sophie.

'Don't go anywhere else. Text me as soon as you're there. We love you, darling. Keep out of sight. Remember they've asked us to stay home.'

Then Sophie was out the door and running.

* * *

The streets were almost empty. A few people were hurrying inside from their cars, holding bags and boxes. One woman was crying and gazing at the sky.

Houses, trees, footpaths all looked ordinary. *Ordinary but changed* – Mr Makereti's word again. Everything's so beautiful, Sophie thought as she raced on. It can't all end. It can't just be wiped out. But somewhere in her mind, she knew it could.

STRANGE MEETING

She stopped for a moment, panting, staring towards the launch site. There in the distance rose the slim, white shape of the Neptune 3 rocket. The rocket that was meant to carry Sunwind into orbit. Would it be destroyed now, like everything else?

Tiny black specks sped around the rocket: vehicles of some sort. Her father was there somewhere, trying to find a way to save them. Had Pita's koro been right? Had space exploration somehow made this happen? It wasn't their fault, surely.

She hurried on to the Makereti's neat little house, and rushed up the path to bang on the front door. Nothing. Nobody.

She hammered on the door again. Where were they? She was shaking again. Any moment now, she'd start to cry.

She grabbed her phone, sent a quick text to her mother. 'I'm okay.' Then she hurried around the back. 'Mr Makereti? Pita? Where are you? Please – '

The door of the little shed was open. Pita stood there, watching her.

THIRTEEN

The boy didn't speak. He jerked his head for her to come in. She stepped into the shed, smelling the fresh wood, feeling the quiet. Pita's granddad stood beside his bench, glasses on the end of his nose. He smiled at Sophie.

She glanced around. The spiny tuatara. The hawk with its great wings spread. And on the bench, something new. A man and woman, heads and shoulders only, faces calm.

But it wasn't the carvings she'd come for. She swallowed, spoke to Pita's koro. 'It's not our fault.'

The man and boy watched her. 'The asteroid.' Her voice shook, but she kept going. 'The space missions. They didn't make this happen.'

Mr Makereti nodded. 'I understand, Sophie. I'm not blaming anyone. Your parents are good people. But there are things in our world nobody can really know. Things it's better to leave alone. That's all.'

Outside on the road, a car tore past. Brakes screeched, and a horn blared. Sophie knew people were trying to hide somehow. But there was nowhere to hide.

Beneath her feet, the ground seemed to tremble for a second. A faint murmur came. She opened her mouth to ask what ... then pointed at the new carving instead.

'They're ... are they ... ?'

Pita was stroking the woman's long hair. 'My Mum and Dad. She looks just like that in the photos.'

Mr Makereti sighed. 'That was my fault. I felt something, but – ' He stopped, then asked, 'Your parents. What are they doing?'

'Dad's at the base. He got a call. Mum's home. She knows I'm here.'

Pita's grandfather nodded. The boy watched

her. I wish I'd really known him, Sophie suddenly thought. Maybe we could have been friends. A shudder ran through her, and she gave a sob. It was too late now.

* * *

Another car engine roared, and brakes screeched again. This time, a door slammed, and feet hurried towards the house. 'Sophie? Mr Makereti?' It was her mother's voice.

Pita stepped outside. Sophie kept gazing at the carving. It was so lovely. So sad.

Mrs Merrill came into the shed. For a moment, she stared at the carvings, too. Then she looked at Pita's koro, and nodded. 'Mr Makereti, this is a special place. I feel ... There's a power here.'

* * *

Still millions of kilometres from Earth the asteroid bores through space, faster and faster. Basements and caves can't protect against something so massive.

It is hurtling 10 times faster than any missile

has ever travelled. It's the speed, the force when it impacts, that will rip the planet open. Faster and faster. One and a half days to go.

* * *

'You are welcome,' Pita's koro told Mrs Merrill. 'The parents of Pita's friend are my friends, too.'

I'm Pita's friend? Sophie thought. Her mother nodded. 'You have been our friend. You gave us a warning. It made people start thinking.'

Mr Makereti sighed. 'I'm sorry it was so late.'

Sophie felt herself shaking again. Everyone was being so polite! The world could end, and they were being nice to one another. Didn't they –

Her mother turned to her. 'I told you a missile can't destroy the asteroid, can't even reach it.'

She paused. 'But that phone call your dad got from the base, saying someone had an idea. It's – '

Everyone in the little shed was listening. And suddenly Sophie knew something else was listening as well. Something great and quiet and calm. Her body tingled. A prickling ran up her back.

Her mum spoke once more. 'There is something that can reach the asteroid.'

Sophie's mouth opened. She and her mother said the word at the same moment.

'Sunwind.'

FOURTEEN

Pita and his koro spoke together.

'How will you do this?' asked the man.

'You gonna put a bomb on it?' asked the boy.

Mrs Merrill shook her head. 'They'll launch Sunwind as soon as they can. Every hour counts now. They'll take it really close to the asteroid, then put the satellite into orbit around it.'

'Yes!' exclaimed Sophie, so loudly that Pita jumped. 'Remember what we talked about in class? Its gravity. The gravity of Sunwind will move the asteroid a tiny bit, maybe change its course. Right Mum? But will it be enough?'

Her mother took her hand, smiled at her. 'You

clever Rocket Girl. Dad says they don't know yet, but every computer at every space centre is working on the calculations.

Mrs Merrill gazed at the other two. 'It's a chance. Maybe the only chance we've got.'

* * *

Mr Makereti took a slow breath. 'You will do this? You will give up your special space mission?'

'This is the most important mission in the world.' Sophie's mother stroked the carving of Pita's parents. 'And you have given up special things, too. Things more important than a space mission.'

The quiet face opposite watched mother and daughter. 'You are indeed good people.'

An engine sounded in the distance. Not a car: something different. Mrs Merrill checked her watch. 'I have to get back. They'll need me at base, for the electronics. Hear that helicopter?' The engine sound was growing louder. 'There are experts flying in from everywhere.'

She gazed at the carvings again. 'Can I ask a

favour? Could Sophie stay with you for a few hours? Or do you want to go to Fatima's, love?'

A look flicked between girl and boy. In spite of the fear that still made her shiver, Sophie felt pleased. 'I'll – I'll stay here.'

'When will you launch your rocket?' Mr Makereti asked.

'They're fuelling it now. They have to be careful: liquid oxygen can explode if there's a mistake. They think ... ' Sophie's mother checked her watch again. 'It's 2.40pm now. They hope to launch – they have to launch no later than nine o'clock tomorrow morning.'

* * *

The colossal rock is charging towards the green and blue planet. The tug of Earth's gravity grows stronger. The asteroid moves faster. Only hours left now.

* * *

Mrs Merrill hugged her daughter. She held Mr Makereti's hand in both of hers. 'Thank you.

Whatever happens, thank you.' Then she was gone. Another helicopter clattered overhead.

'Pita,' his koro said softly. 'Would you take Sophie inside the house? I'd like to be by myself for a little.'

Pita nodded. As he and Sophie began moving towards the house, Sophie heard Mr Makereti's voice again. Or was it him? Was it ...

'You want to walk somewhere?' the boy asked. 'I don't want to just sit inside.'

They headed down the front path to the footpath. A few cars still passed, but they seemed quieter. Groups of people stood outside houses. Some had their arms around each other.

'What you gonna do when you finish school?' Pita's words made her jerk. This was crazy. Would they ever go to school again? But she heard herself speak and felt pleased her voice was steady. 'Dunno. Space research, maybe. How about you?'

'Real Rocket Girl, eh?' The boy's eyes were on the ground. 'I'll be like my koro, if I can. Carving wood. Or maybe planting trees, like Mum and Dad

STRANGE MEETING

did. Be great to be like them. Better than any silly space stuff.'

Sophie glared, then saw the faint grin on the boy's face. She said nothing. She couldn't. A wave of love for her own mother and father was sweeping through her.

I might never grow up, she knew. In a few days, I might not even be alive. But if I do grow up, if we survive, I'm going to live the very best life I can.

* * *

When they reached the corner they could see Mahoe Launch Site, out across the flat land. A white vapour rose from the rocket, and drifted away on the breeze. The fuelling, Sophie thought.

Behind the launch pad, a small plane came buzzing in to land. More experts, Sophie realised. Experts like Mum and Dad. I don't just love them, she thought; I'm proud of them, too.

'Tell me again,' Pita asked. 'How's that thing gonna stop an asteroid? It's too small to do anything, isn't it?'

'It won't stop it,' Sophie reminded him. 'Its weight, its gravity might change the asteroid's direction a tiny bit. If they're in time and the asteroid is still far enough away, it might just be enough to make it miss the earth.'

Again, she couldn't believe how calm she sounded while her stomach was churning and her heart pounded. It has to work, she thought. Please!

FIFTEEN

Can the tiny satellite do this? The vast rock flashes on, straight towards the planet that turns slowly ahead of it.

If it hits, it will hit with the force of a billion nuclear bombs. The closer it gets, the less time there is for anything to change its course. It's not just days or hours that matter now. It's minutes.

* * *

Sophie and Pita wandered around a few other streets. What if I meet any other kids from school? Sophie thought. And why am I worrying about that at a time like this?

She texted Fatima: 'U OK? Walking w Pita.' Back

came a reply: 'Tell me some time. C U @ school ... I hope. U OK 2?'

School ... If we survive this, I'll be happy to do the most boring lessons forever.

She and Pita talked about kids in their class and about Mahoe itself. When they got back to his place, Mr Makereti was still in his shed, with the door closed.

Sophie twitched as the ground seemed to murmur again. No, this time it was her phone vibrating. It was her mum, 'Coming home. CU there.'

'I gotta go,' she told Pita. They gazed at each other for a moment, then looked away. No sound from the shed.

Then the ground did stir, ever so faintly. Pita spoke. 'My koro hasn't given up yet.'

As she started home, fear crawling inside her again, Sophie tried to understand what he had meant.

* * *

She was partway home when she stopped. She

stood hugging herself, shaking with fright. Nine o'clock tomorrow morning. The only chance to save everyone and everything. Pita was right: the rocket and its satellite were so tiny, how could they ...

She began running; sprinting along the footpath, terror swelling inside her once more. We can't all be killed, she told herself. We can't! But it happened to the dinosaurs, so big and powerful. It can happen to us.

She raced up the path, flung open the door, threw herself into her mother's arms. Tears streamed down her face. 'Mum, it'll be all right, won't it? Please?'

Mrs Merrill held her tight. 'The best brains in the world are working on it, love. Your father's coming home later. He'll tell us if there's anything new.'

Mother and daughter made themselves eat something. They talked. They watched TV, as the expert explained what Sunwind hoped to do. The Prime Minister came on again, half smiled, told people to stay calm and look after one another. Was the rest of the world as calm as people here seemed to be? Sophie wondered. They seemed to be: there were no reports of riots. Maybe everyone is just waiting and hoping.

For an hour, they looked at old photo albums. 'You were such a cute kid.' Her mother hugged her again. 'You still are.'

Mr Merrill's car swept up the drive. Sophie's father kissed his wife and daughter. 'They're launching early,' he said straightaway. 'Countdown's all going smoothly; no weird radar shapes or power cuts this time, so they're launching as soon as they can. Every half hour helps now.'

'Dad?' Sophie knew her voice was shaking. 'It'll work, won't it? It'll stop the asteroid hitting us?'

Her father gazed at her. 'You're a brave girl, love. I'm so proud of you. The answer is – we don't know. It's got a chance. The sooner we get it up, the better that chance is.'

He stopped for a second. 'If it can't move the asteroid by flying near, they might crash Sunwind into it, to see if they can knock it a tiny fraction. Only if nothing else works.'

He put his arms around his daughter and wife again. 'We've done everything we can. Now we wait and see.'

* * *

Sophie had no idea if she slept. She lay in bed, staring at the ceiling, listening to her parents talking quietly and moving around the house. More helicopters clattered overhead. Out in the streets, people walked past. Everyone seemed to be awake this night. The last night of their lives, maybe.

She thought of Sunwind, all the amazing things it could have learned and done. Of Mahoe Launch Site, her parents and all their work.

And she thought of Mr Makereti and his grandson, maybe awake a few streets away. Was he still in that little shed? Could he somehow...? She hardly knew what she meant.

If we survive this, if we stay alive and I can grow up, I'm going to try and understand all sorts of things, she promised herself. Science is awesome, but there are other things, too. If I – terror swept through her again. She hugged herself and tried to breathe slowly.

When her phone showed 6am, she got up and went through to the living room, where her parents sat in front of the TV.

* * *

The huge rock's speed builds and builds. Its black, scarred surface flashes through space. It makes no noise now, but if it enters Earth's atmosphere, it will roar and bellow as it plunges down.

When it hits the surface, the explosion will be so loud, it will burst eardrums thousands of kilometres away.

It weighs 500 billion trillion tonnes.

Millions of miles away Sunwind glows in the moonlight. It weighs just 60 tonnes. What chance has the little speck of metal got? Yet it's Earth's only hope.

SIXTEEN

'Do you want anything to eat, love?' Sophie's mum asked. Sophie shook her head.

'We'll watch the launch from out on the road,' Mr Merrill said. 'Seems more real that way.'

For half an hour, they sat together on the couch. On their TV, the Neptune 3 glowed in the launch pad's lights, the barrel-shaped satellite perched on its tip. Can that little thing really change the path of an asteroid? Sophie wondered. It's got to.

Vapour drifted from the Neptune's great first-stage rockets. One last vehicle, a tanker of some sort, stood beside the slim, white shape. Then it drove away.

At 6.36 am Sophie's father stood. 'Let's go. Bring your jacket, love.'

Outside, the sky was still dark, though an orange streak showed along the horizon. Shadowy groups of people moved towards the corner. Many held hands. Some were crying. I'm not afraid, Sophie thought. I may be later, but I'm not afraid. I'm going to see everything I can. I'm not going to waste a second.

Mr Makereti and Pita were already standing at the corner. Pita's koro shook hands with all of them. 'This is a fine thing you are doing,' he told Sophie's parents.

In the distance, the rocket stood unmoving. Launch-pad lights still glowed, but daylight was growing. 6.47 am.

A man in the crowd must have recognised Mr and Mrs Merrill. 'How long will it take,' he asked, 'to reach the asteroid?'

'Maybe four hours.' Sophie's dad sounded as calm as if he was giving a lecture. 'Depends how fast the asteroid is travelling. It's speeding up all the time as it gets closer, so it's hard to measure its velocity for sure. They'll fly as close as they can, then go into a tight orbit.'

'It's going to be on the TV,' Sophie's mother added. 'They'll track it all the way.'

Nobody spoke.

6.52 am. 6.54 am.

Sophie's parents had their arms around each other. Her mum pulled her close.

6.56 am. 6.58 am.

The siren blared. Once, twice, three times. Sophie's body went rigid. Blast-off in one minute.

* * *

A thicker mist grew around the Neptune 3's base. Fuel pumps, forcing liquid oxygen towards the engines. The rocket stood, lean and white and still.

Someone nearby had a radio. '40 ... 39 ... 38,' a voice sounded. 'Fuel pumps off. 31 ... 30 ... 29. We have go for main engine start. 22 ... 21 ... 20. Main engine ignition. 16 ... 15 ... 14 ... '

Something black and skinny swung away from the rocket. 'Power cables,' Sophie's dad breathed. A shimmering grew around the white shape.

Orange flame poured from the ground. Jets of fire were pouring into the blast pit beneath the rocket. White smoke billowed halfway up the launch tower. A deep rumbling reached the watching crowd.

'Four ... three ... two ... one. We have lift-off!' Somehow, the tall launch tower was sliding down into the ground. No, it was the Neptune 3, rising up beside it, standing on a pillar of red and orange fire that streamed from its base.

For a second, it seemed to hang beside the tower. Then it slowly rose upwards, an arrow flashing into the morning sky.

* * *

The distant bellow of engines faded. The rocket was already a tiny white shape, high in the sky when there was a flicker, and something seemed to drop from it. The first-stage rockets, falling away, floating on parachutes back to the ground. The satellite sped on.

People were exclaiming. A few even clapped. A few others sobbed.

Mr Makereti spoke. 'Thank you,' he said to Sophie's parents. 'You have done something very fine. I pray it works.'

Sophie's dad nodded. 'Now we wait.'

Silence, then Pita went 'Koro?' When Sophie glanced at the boy's grandfather, she saw a look on his face that she'd never seen before.

'Yes,' murmured Mr Makereti. 'Yes, we wait.'

But he's not going to wait. Sophie felt sure, for some reason. He's going to do something else.

SEVENTEEN

A text pinged for Sophie's mum as they walked home. 'They need me at the base to help with satellite data. Your Dad will look after you, love. You look after him.'

The streets were quiet. I should be going to school, Sophie realised. But schools were all closed – and anyway, who would be going to school when … when the world might be about to end?

The words still didn't seem real. Her body hunched for a moment, her stomach churned. But she couldn't really believe.

She and her father ate breakfast in front of the TV. Sophie hardly noticed what she put in her mouth. The screen showed Mahoe Launch Centre (the whole world is watching us, Sophie thought) and numbers streaming past. The speed of the satellite: its engines were flinging it away from Earth as fast as possible. Other figures showed the shrinking distance between the satellite and the asteroid. Mr Merrill explained it all. 'We can track its position and direction; we're estimating its speed, as best we can.'

There were no shots of Sunwind itself. No camera on Earth could show the little shape hurtling into space.

A voice spoke from the screen. A technician somewhere. 'Contact in three hours.'

* * *

It's a race now. Huge asteroid and tiny satellite, speeding towards each other.

At Mahoe Launch Control, eyes stare at computer screens. Fingers move on keyboards. The distance between target and missile shrinks with every second. Closer. And closer.

* * *

9.20am. A car swished into the driveway. 'They sent me home.' Sophie's mother tried to smile. 'Your dad and I have done our bit.'

Again, Sophie felt so proud of her parents. Why couldn't people be brave and clever like this all the time?

She sat, stood, walked around, went out to the footpath. She started towards the Makereti's house, then stopped. No. Pita's koro had to be alone just now. Somehow, she knew that.

'Sophie?' She swung around. It was Fatima and her parents. 'We are just walking,' said Fatima's mother. 'The world is so beautiful. Thank you, Sophie. You have been a wonderful friend to my daughter.'

She hugged Sophie. So did Fatima. There were tears on both girls' faces.

One and a half hours to go.

* * *

Sunwind's sensors have found the asteroid. Its on-

board computers flash the recognition. It alters course.

Satellite and rock hurtle towards each other at a combined speed of 40 kilometres per second, a speed that grows even faster as the Earth gets nearer. Sunwind must skim past the asteroid as closely as it can, then swing into the tightest possible orbit. Only then can its 60 tonnes have any effect. Will that be enough? Nobody knows.

Maybe one hour to go.

* * *

The Merrills sat close together on the couch, eyes locked on the TV.

Numbers streamed past. Numbers that grew smaller and smaller as the distance shrank. A voice was counting. '20 minutes till fly-past ... 18 minutes till fly-past. Asteroid velocity increasing: revised time 15 minutes.'

Outside, the streets were silent. Sophie's parents had their arms around her. '13 minutes to fly-past ... Revised time: 11 minutes.'

Sophie's stomach churned. Her heart thumped. '10 minutes ... nine minutes ... ' She felt a sob in her throat. Please, she begged silently. Please. 'Seven minutes ... six minutes ...'

Save us, Sunwind. Save us! The words beat in her head. 'Four minutes ... three minutes ... '

Her parents' arms tightened around her. She squeezed her eyes shut. 'Two minutes ... one minute ... 30 seconds ...'

The voice changed. 'Fly-past!'

The sob burst from Sophie's mouth. She opened her eyes, and stared at the TV.

A different voice spoke. 'No change.'

Her mother's body jerked beside her. 'It's too early to tell. Too early!'

The first voice again. 'Orbit established.' A pause, then the second voice. 'No change.'

Figures kept streaming down the screen. The first voice had gone silent. Only the second voice spoke, as seconds ticked by.

'No change ... No change ...'

STRANGE MEETING

Her parents sat rigid. More seconds passed. 'No change ... No change ... '

So suddenly that Sophie gasped, her father snatched the remote, and turned off their TV. He and his wife gazed at each other, and then at their daughter.

Her mum placed a hand against Sophie's cheek. 'I'm so sorry, darling. It's not working. It's not enough.'

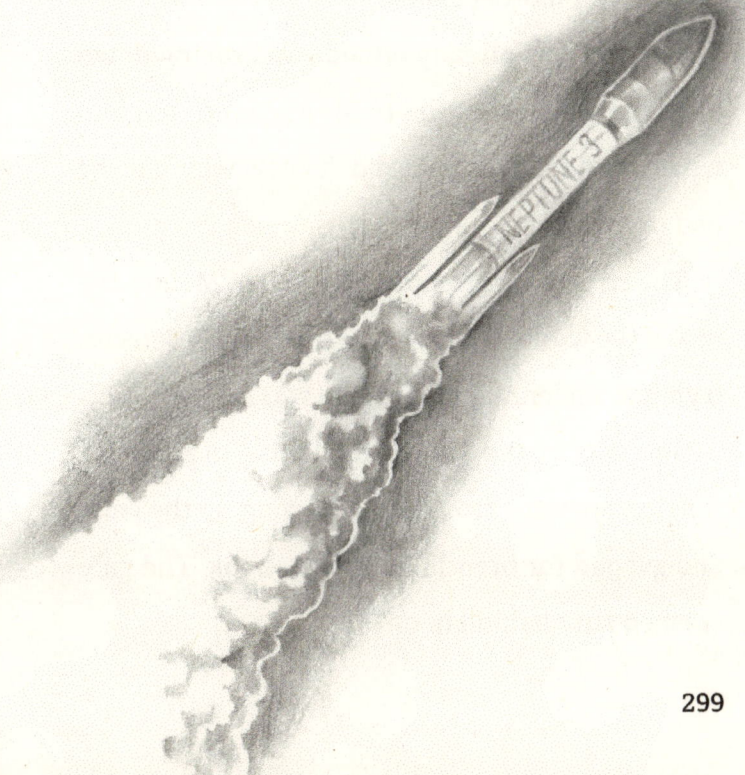

EIGHTEEN

Sophie leaped up and rushed for the door. 'Darling, what – ' her mother called.

But she was already outside and racing down the path. She had to get to Mr Makereti, tell him what was happening. She didn't know why, but she had to go.

The streets were empty. The rest of Mahoe, the rest of the world maybe, were staring at TV screens, trying to understand that there was no hope.

She was at the Makeretis' house in minutes, flinging open the front gate, charging up the path. She gasped for breath, her body shook. The gate crashed shut behind her.

STRANGE MEETING

She tore around the side of the house, and straight into someone. Pita. He grabbed her as she nearly fell.

'Sunwind!' Sophie panted. 'It's not going to work. It's not enough. I – '

Pita held her arms. 'I know,' he went. 'So does my koro.'

Sophie was still shaking. No, it wasn't her. The ground had begun to tremble. Pita gripped her arms harder.

'I want to – to see him.' The earth under her feet shuddered again. A low murmuring began.

Pita shook his head. 'He told me to go. Stay out of the shed. He has to be alone.'

'Why does he – ' Sophie stopped. Her heart seemed to stop, too. The murmuring swelled to a hum. A voice was speaking. Many voices, deep and quiet.

Light began to pour from the ground. Golden light, beautiful, clear, glowing like the Sun. It streamed skywards, all around them. From the little shed where Mr Makereti was, it flowed up, even brighter and richer. It was calm and gentle, yet it sped into the blue morning air faster than anything Sophie had ever seen.

She heard herself shouting. Pita's arms were around her. Then he cried out also. And Sophie saw.

* * *

Faces had appeared in the glow. One ... two ... 10 ... more and more. Faces that watched her and Pita, watched the world around them, while the golden light poured on.

Some were old, from long, long ago, Sophie felt sure. Some were human. Some were more than human, somehow. They were calm and silent, and full of power, just like the light.

Pita's body jerked, and he called out again.

Sophie saw them at the same time. A man and a woman, the ones from the carving, there in the middle of the golden glow. For a few seconds they gazed at her and Pita, seemed to smile at the boy.

Then they and the great light were gone, flashing

upwards. In half a second, they had vanished into the sky.

* * *

'What's happened?' Sophie tried to understand. Something wonderful, that was all she knew.

Pita still held her. She started to pull away, towards the little shed. Around them, the garden lay silent and empty.

'Leave him!' Pita said. 'Leave him! Your place – quick!' Like runners in some crazy race, the two of them sprinted for the Merrills' house.

* * *

Her mother and father were still in the living room. But they were standing now. Standing and staring at the TV screen, where numbers continued to stream past.

A voice was shouting from the screen as the two kids burst in. 'Unknown ... incredible!'

'Sophie!' her mother gasped. 'Something's happened. Listen!'

The voice from the TV kept shouting. 'Instruments

can't explain it! ... A cloud of some sort ... A force field ... the speed of light ... surrounding Sunwind!'

The numbers on screen changed: smaller in some places, bigger in others. The voice stopped, started again. Sophie's mother and father were shouting, too.

'Lateral movement!' the screen voice yelled. 'The asteroid is shifting ... Wait ... Yes, movement confirmed ... 20 metres ... 50 metres ... It's on a new course!'

Sophie couldn't hear any more, because her parents had grabbed her and Pita, were shaking and hugging them at the same time. Her mother was laughing and gasping.

'It's happened, Sophie! Whatever it was, it's worked. The asteroid's going to miss Earth. We're saved, love! We're saved!'

NINETEEN

The great rock is changing course. The tiny spacecraft, and the golden glow surrounding it, are pulling at the asteroid, moving it.

It slides sideways, a few metres, then a few metres more. The glow fades, then strengthens again, pouring towards the asteroid. The huge shape moves further.

Earth isn't straight in front any more. It's off to one side, just a tiny fraction. But that's enough.

Beyond the green and blue planet lies the blackness of deep space. Stars glitter, hundreds of light years away. The asteroid's new path is set. It will skim past Earth, then glide far into space, disappearing into that darkness.

The golden glow is fading. Slowly, it dims. One last time, it surrounds Sunwind; then it is gone.

The tiny satellite drifts on, too, away from the asteroid, away from its home. Its mission is over. A different mission from what it was built for but a mission far more wonderful.

While around satellite, asteroid and planet, the great wheel of the Milky Way Galaxy slowly turns.

* * *

Mr Merrill drove Pita home. It took a while, he told them when he got back, because the streets were jammed with people, cheering, laughing, crying. 'Pity we can't be like that all the time,' he said. Sophie remembered thinking the same thing.

Her mother hugged Pita before he left. So did Sophie. She and the boy didn't look at each other afterwards.

'Mr Makereti's an amazing man, all right,' Sophie's father said as he gazed at his daughter. 'Something happened there, didn't it, love?'

'Yeah,' Sophie went. 'Yeah, it did.'

* * *

She knew she wouldn't sleep. Who could, on this day when the world had been saved? Saved in a way she might never understand. That glow. Those faces. She'd never forget them. She'd been a part of something beautiful.

She lay in bed, staring at the ceiling. She closed her eyes, heard herself yawn, then opened her eyes again as somebody turned the light on.

Bright morning sunshine was streaming into her bedroom.

* * *

Was there school today? Who cares? Sophie thought.

Was there work today? 'Who cares?' her parents said.

The Prime Minister was on TV, speaking about their marvellous escape. She paused, then said, 'Something very special happened in our country yesterday. Not just what Sunwind did, though we're so proud of that. Something else that we don't understand yet. Whatever it was, we'll always be grateful for what it did.'

After breakfast, they walked around to the Makeretis' house because 'There are things I need to ask,' Mr Merrill had said.

Pita and his granddad were on the back lawn. The man smiled at them. 'Welcome, friends. I'm just telling this boy it's time he cut the grass.'

He looks tired, Sophie thought. Tired but ... peaceful.

'Come and see what I've been doing.' Mr Makereti opened the door of his shed.

Inside the little building, she stared in amazement. A new carving stood on the bench. A flame rising from the ground like a glowing fire, soaring upwards, shapes half showing inside.

But another carving had gone. The figures of Pita's mother and father weren't there.

Sophie swallowed. I'll never really know what happened, she thought. And that's okay.

Her mum was gazing at the carvings. 'How do you think of these things?'

Pita's koro touched the flame. 'I don't. Something else does the thinking for me.'

He nodded towards Pita, who stood watching him proudly. 'I keep telling this young fellow. We live in a special place. A place of power. If we're careful, and if we're lucky, we can use this power to do great things.'

Sophie's father nodded. 'All my life, I've tried to understand how things happen. I don't think I'll ever know what happened here. You're right, Mr Makereti. Sometimes it's best to leave things that way.'

Pita's grandfather smiled. 'And sometimes your way is best. Both ways worked together yesterday and that is best of all.'

Sophie was still staring at the carved flame, with the shapes inside. How did he do that so fast? Did he do it? She'd probably never know what her question meant, or the answer to it. That was okay, too.

Before she knew it, she smiled at Pita. The boy smiled back. That's definitely okay, she decided.

'Come and have dinner with us,' her mother was saying. 'Both of you. There's so much to talk about.'

'Yes, please come,' Mr Merrill added. 'There are things I want to do, and you can help me, I'm sure.'

Pita's koro smiled. 'We should ask these two young ones what they want to do, as well. You're still going to be Rocket Girl, Sophie?'

'I ... yes,' Sophie paused. 'Or maybe a carver.'

The three adults laughed. 'How about you, Pita?' asked Sophie's mum.

'A carver,' went Pita, just as he had before. Then he smiled at Sophie again. 'Or maybe a Rocket Boy.'

ABOUT THE AUTHOR
DAVID HILL

PHOTOGRAPHER: Robert Cross, Victoria University of Wellington

David Hill lives in Taranaki, and has been a full time author for 40 years. He writes fiction and non-fiction for most age groups. His novels and stories for YA and younger readers have won various awards, and are published in some 15 countries and almost as many languages.